AFTER THE TEMPEST

LORRAINE BARTLETT

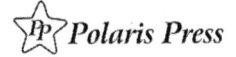

Polaris Press

After The Tempest (Lotus Bay Mystery #5)

COPYRIGHT © 2025 by Lorraine Bartlett. All rights reserved.

No part of this book may be reproduced in any form by any electronic or mechanical means (including photocopying, recording, or information storage and retrieval) without permission in writing from the author.

This is a work of fiction. Names, characters, places, and incidents are either the product of the author's imagination, or are used fictitiously, and any resemblance to actual persons, living or dead, is purely coincidental.

No generative artificial intelligence (AI) was used in the writing of this work. The author expressly prohibits any entity from using this publication for purposes of training AI technologies to generate text, including without limitation technologies that are capable of generating works in the same style or genre as this publication. The author reserves all rights to license uses of this work for generative AI training and development of machine learning language models.

Publisher's Note: The recipes contained in this ebook should be followed as written. The publisher is not responsible for any adverse reactions to the recipes contained in this book.

Cover by Wicked Smart Designs.

❦ Created with Vellum

ACKNOWLEDGMENTS

My thanks go to:

The members of The Lorraine Train: Amy Connolley, Debbie Lyon, Pam Priest, and Kim Templeton for their continued support.

Join my private Facebook Group Page, Lorraine's & Lorna's (cozy) Perpetual Tea Party.

DESCRIPTION

After a violent rainstorm passes over Lotus Bay, Tori Cannon notices that her friend Anissa's boat is missing from her marina. The women go in search of the craft only to find it floating loose —with a dead man inside who was apparently electrocuted, casting suspicion on Anissa. While Tori tries to figure out what happened, her BFF and roommate, Kathy Grant, has money problems, forcing her to take a job as a server at The Bay Bar. Tori's navigating her own financial challenges, so she must take a break from sleuthing to return to substitute teaching. But when a gridiron bully takes a swing at her, she's left battered and bruised —and unable to work.

Can Kathy's score of a last-minute bridal shower at her B&B save the day? Will Tori's sleuthing uncover how (and why) the dead man died? Find out in *After The Tempest!*

CAST OF CHARACTERS

Tori Cannon, owner of Cannon's Bait & Tackle
Kathy Grant, owner of Swans Nest Inn and Tori's best friend
Anissa Jackson, contractor and Tori's childhood friend
Herb Cannon, Tori's paternal grandfather
Noreen Darcy, co-owner of The Bay Bar and Paul's wife
Paul Darcy, co-owner of The Bay Bar and Noreen's husband
Detective Osborn, a member of the Ward County Sheriff's Department
Eric Mooney, Tori's and Anissa's neighbor
Alice Stanton, wife of electrocution victim
Barb Smith, Paul Darcy's sister
Chuck Stanton, electrocution victim
Lucinda Bloomfield, richest woman in Ward County and Anissa's neighbor

CHAPTER 1

When the sky darkened to the north, you knew a storm was brewing. Tori Cannon turned her binocular-aided gaze toward Lotus Point and could barely make out the pier where splotches of white indicated the waves crashing over the cement walkway leading to the lighthouse. Lowering the glasses, she ran from the grassy patch in front of her empty bait shop to the bungalow she shared with her best friend forever, Kathy Grant, to close the windows. She didn't need her floors and furniture soaked by the rain that was sure to hit within ten or so minutes. The cats always freaked out when a storm hit, and the weather that blanketed the bay from the north could be fierce.

Once the house was secure, Tori hurried back to Cannon's Bait & Tackle to see the empty slips off her dock fill as fishermen made it back to shore before the tempest hit.

Always fascinated by how rapidly the weather on the bay could change, Tori watched the downpour advance like a thick gray curtain, which always made her gut tighten. This was not the usual cloudburst. Instead, the sky turned black, and the gusts became as ferocious as she'd ever seen, causing waves to crash over her breakwall and sending the boats in their slips bouncing in the roiling water. The wind began to howl like a banshee with a toothache, and a couple of her regulars sought refuge in her cement block shop rather than retreating to their cars.

"You ever see it this bad on the bay?" Mike Louis asked, sounding breathless. He was soaked to the skin, his salt-and-pepper hair plastered against his skull.

Tori shook her head and returned to her stool behind the sales counter. "Not in all the summers I've been on the bay."

"I sure hope I tied my boat securely," said Todd Brewster, wiping droplets off his face. "I'd hate for it to sink in this gale."

The three of them watched the storm intensify with bolts of lightning fracturing the sky as it grew in fury, heading toward Lotus Bay's southern shore, the sound of the wind growing in decibels.

Leaves from the big willow and several maples on the property began to whip around the bait shop like green snowflakes, and yet Tori knew the squall would blow over in a short time. Sometimes, the rain came in waves so that the sun would peek out as though it were in the eye of a hurricane before the onslaught would begin again. But now the rain pounded even harder until Tori could only see a few of the boats in the slips encircling her docks bobbing on the wind-swept waves.

Then, through the raging rivulets of water drenching the bait shop windows, Tori saw a form in a yellow slicker approach. The door was wrenched open, sending in a chilly blast before the wind caught it, slamming it shut again.

Tori's childhood friend and contractor, Anissa Jackson, pulled the slicker's hood off her head, shaking out her wiry curls. "It's not a fit day for man nor beast."

"And you happen to be neither," Tori pointed out nervously.

The slicker had only kept Anissa's upper body dry. Her denim overalls were soaked from the knees down, and her face was dripping as well.

"Why didn't you wait for the storm to pass before you came over here?" Tori asked.

Anissa had been working on the upper level of Tori's boathouse. She was in the midst of turning that rustic loft into a luxury suite that Tori would be able to rent out for top dollar… eventually. As they were past Labor Day weekend, the market for such accommodations had petered out. Anissa estimated another week or two to finish the suite. That is if she didn't get other work. It didn't matter. Tori hadn't planned to rent the place until the following summer, anyway.

As though by magic, the pounding rain slackened, and the western shore began to emerge from the mist. Anissa shook her head. "I'll never get over how fast the weather changes around here."

"Me, either," Tori said.

"I'm heading home," Todd said.

"Me, too," Mike echoed, and the men left the bait shop for the parking lot.

Tori turned her attention back to the piece of broken china she'd been shaping into a heart with a Dremel. When the bait business was slow, she made pendants to sell to her customers, not that she'd had that many in-person sales. Fingers crossed, come November, she hoped to see an influx of orders from her online shop. Once the Tuesday after Labor Day rolled around, those looking to buy bait evaporated like the puddles in her parking lot after a downpour. Anissa gazed through the window that overlooked the docks and swore. "Damn. My boat's gone."

Tori rose from her seat to have a look. "You're right. It must have broken loose during the storm. We can go retrieve it with one of mine."

"Now?"

Tori shrugged. "I'm not exactly drowning in customers. Now that the weather's calmed down, I can close for the few minutes it'll take to tow it back."

Tori hung a BE RIGHT BACK sign on the bait shop's door and locked it. But as the women headed down the wet dock to one of the business's rentals, there was no sign of Anissa's dinghy out on the bay.

"Where's my boat? That storm only lasted about fifteen minutes, and the wind came from the north. Do you think it got blown under the bay bridge to the marsh next to Kathy?"

Kathy and Tori met on their first day at SUNY Brockport and had been BFFs ever since. Kathy had a degree in hotel management and now owned a bed and breakfast—Swans Nest—right across the street from Cannon's Bait & Tackle.

Tori grabbed her phone, tapping Kathy's name on the contacts list. "Hey, Kath—can you look out the window to see if there's a boat outside your place? Anissa's has gone missing."

"Just a minute."

It was more than a minute later when Kathy spoke again. "I went outside. No boats by my place."

"Thanks." Tori pocketed her phone once again.

The worst of the mist had lifted, and the islands had reappeared to the north. "I don't see anything sitting out in the bay. What do you think happened to it?" Anissa asked.

"I dunno. Hang on, and I'll get the binoculars." Tori retrieved them from the bait shop and locked the door once again. She rejoined Anissa on the dock and scanned the shore to the west. Nothing. They'd have to get on the water to search the eastern side of the bay.

Tori handed the binoculars to Anissa and wished she'd grabbed a towel as they hopped into the boat and sat on the cold, wet seat. "Ewww."

"My butt wasn't wet, so now it'll match my pantslegs," Anissa said, taking a seat in the bow.

Tori cast off and let the boat drift a few feet before starting the motor. The little vessel took off, leaving a small wake as it plowed through the rippling water.

Anissa twisted like a pretzel, the binoculars pressed to her face. As Tori steered the ten-foot aluminum boat's twelve-horsepower motor, she saw no point in warning her friend that she'd get a stiff neck. Because of the motor's roar, there was no way she'd be heard.

They'd passed Fisher's Point when Anissa lowered the glasses. Tori saw a craft up ahead. "Is that it?" she asked and pointed.

"Those are my registration numbers," Anissa hollered, sounding elated.

As they approached the boat, Tori could see the frayed rope that had attached the boat to one of the slips on her dock. The storm had done a number on it all right. She set the motor to trolling speed and noticed something else—a tarp?—was mounded in the middle of the small dingy.

Suddenly, Anissa stood, causing the boat to wobble dangerously.

"Anissa!" Tori admonished, abandoning the tiller to grasp the sides of the boat in an effort to steady it *and* herself.

Anissa plunked down, but it was obvious something was terribly wrong.

"What is it?" Tori asked.

"I think," Anissa began, "there's somebody in *my* boat!"

"What?" Tori had to fight the urge to stand to take a look and sat up straighter, straining to see into the boat. The mound still looked like a tarp to her. She steered the boat closer. Anissa grabbed what was left of the rope and pulled the boat close. The women peered into it.

Under the blue plastic tarp was a man squashed into the space between the seats. His mouth was open, a horrific expression covering his face, and his filmy, open eyes were fixed on the sky above.

Tori swallowed. She'd seen dead men before, and this guy had recently joined that club. "Do you recognize him?" she asked, feeling squeamish.

"No, but his hands," Anissa said, aghast.

"What's wrong with them?"

"They're black."

Tori didn't understand. She'd thought the guy was Caucasian. "You mean like yours?"

"No, it's a white guy—but his hands are...charred."

Tori's stomach did a flip-flop. "Holy crap."

"You've got that right," Anissa said. "What is a dead guy with burned hands doing in *my* boat? How am I going to explain this to the po-lice? Especially if they send out that disagreeable Detective Osborn."

Tori swallowed. The Ward County Sheriff's detective was *not* one of her favorite people. He seemed to take it as a personal affront whenever he was called to the Cannon Compound.

"Are you sure he's dead?" Tori asked, dreading the answer.

"Deader than a doornail," Anissa said, sounding less than thrilled. It was the first time Anissa had encountered a body. Tori had twice had the honor of that distinction. Still, Anissa hadn't panicked, which said a lot.

"I'd better call nine one one," Tori said, and pulled her phone from her pocket. She had good service thanks to the cell tower on the ridge nearby and in seconds was speaking with the Ward County 911 dispatcher.

"We'll be towing the boat and the body to Cannon's Bait & Tackle at Ridge and Resort Roads." When she ended the call, she pocketed the phone once again and cast about until she found a couple of bungee cords.

"You expect to tow my boat with those?" Anissa asked skeptically.

"We've got nothing else."

Anissa shook her head, but made a square knot to hold the cords together, and snagged and tied them to the front of the dingy. Anissa took her seat again, looking perturbed as they started back south again.

"I wish I didn't have to look at a dead body all the way back to your place."

"Then you'd better shut your eyes," Tori said reasonably, even if she didn't feel quite that calm.

~

THE PARKING LOT was riddled with puddles—some of them pretty deep—when the cops showed up at the Cannon compound. They took a look at the dead guy in the boat and immediately called for backup. It was then Tori was convinced that any plans she held for the evening were effectively squashed. Anissa was even more upset. That a dead white guy was found in her boat had her conjuring up all sorts of scenarios—and none of them were good.

The women answered the same questions over and over again as twilight darkened the sky. Neither of them had had supper, and Anissa's stomach growled loudly. Tori's tummy wasn't any happier. Finally, Tori's housemate, Kathy, arrived at the compound to inquire just what was going on.

"My boat escaped in the storm," Anissa said simply. "And there's a *dead* guy in it!"

"Do you know who it is?" Kathy asked, her eyes wide.

"Haven't got a clue," Tori answered. "We're hungry. Any chance you could whip us up something to eat? Maybe the cops would let us leave to eat our dinner," she said pointedly with a glance at one of the uniformed deputies. They were waiting for a detective to show up—and the medical examiner from Rochester. Ward County, in rural New York, couldn't afford such an official.

"You should stay here. And you ladies shouldn't be speaking to each other," one of the deputies said, looking at Tori and Anissa.

Tori knew he didn't want them contaminating each other's stories. But the thing was, they had no stories.

"Look, deputy, we've told you what happened and what we

saw. And I'm just guessing, but the fact that the guy's hands are burned leads me to believe he may have been electrocuted—and not in Anissa's boat."

"And why would you believe that?" the deputy asked suspiciously.

Tori spoke slowly, just in case the guy was a little dim. "Because his hands are burned," she repeated. "Charred, more like. There's no electricity near Anissa's slip, and neither of us has ever seen him before."

The deputy still looked at them with suspicion. "You'll have to wait until the detective gets here. In the meantime, I'd appreciate it if you ladies would sit in separate areas." He gestured toward the vintage metal chairs that lined the bank overlooking the bay. The ones Tori had sanded the rust from and painted in bright, primary colors.

"Can our friend at least bring us something to eat?" Anissa asked. "I'm about ready to eat my foot—with or without barbecue sauce."

The deputy looked at her as though she'd grown a second head.

"Kath, please," Tori pleaded.

With a quick nod, Kathy disappeared, heading toward the bungalow.

Ten minutes later, Tori and Anissa were munching breakfast sandwiches of sausage patties, cheese, and egg on buttered English muffins when Detective Osborn of the Ward County Sheriff's Department arrived, looking distinctly annoyed to be called out after hours.

"And what trouble have you ladies gotten yourselves into now?" the detective asked sourly.

He looked like a G-man from the 1970s with his close-cropped fair hair and his belligerent posture. Still, after putting up with the whims of the deputies for more than an hour after a long stint womaning the bait shop, Tori had just about run out of patience for the day. Still, knowing how the law was apt to treat her African American friend, Tori was determined to protect Anissa from an unfair justice system that often seemed ambivalent to truth, justice, and the American way.

"I'll speak to you first," Osborn said to Tori as she took a last bite of her sandwich. "Was that sausage I smell?"

Tori nodded. "Walmart's finest turkey sausage patty," she told him. She and Kathy did a run to the nearest super center once a month to stock up on vital things like fifty-pound sacks of cat litter, baking supplies for Kathy's B&B, and cheap chicken wings for the air fryer.

"Would you like a breakfast sandwich?" Kathy asked the detective. "I can whip one up for you in just a couple of minutes."

He looked like he'd like to answer in the affirmative but instead shook his head, looking wistful.

Osborn led Tori away from Anissa and the deputies, who seemed to have nothing better to do than stand around, not doing much, and looking like they might want to pose for a hot-cop calendar. This lot was young. The older guys probably got the daytime shifts.

"When did Ms. Jackson's boat go missing?" Osborn asked Tori.

She thought about it. "I really can't say. For all I know, it could have been days."

"You don't keep track of who comes and goes in your marina?"

"Last I heard, we still live in a free country, Detective. People come and go as they please."

"But this boat, in particular, belongs to your close friend."

"Yeah, but I don't keep track of it."

"Why not?"

"I don't keep track of *any* boat in my marina. If my customers pay, they pay for the month or the season, whether they use the slip or not."

"And your friend…how much does she pay you?"

"Nothing."

"And why's that?"

"Because not only is Anissa my friend, but she's also my contractor. She's building an apartment over my old boat house."

"Is the perk you give her something that should be reported to the IRS?"

"What?"

"You're giving her a perk that's worth hundreds of dollars."

"Yeah, and if my water pipes burst in the middle of the night in January she comes and fixes them and doesn't charge me a nickel. It's called friendship, Detective. You might want to try it sometime," Tori said acidly.

Osborn just glared at her.

"What happens next?" Tori asked.

"We try to identify the dead man."

"Correct me if I'm wrong, but that might be hard to do without fingerprints. With those burned hands, I'm pretty sure the dead guy has none."

"Fingerprints are only one form of identification. And they'd only be on file if the deceased was a criminal or at one time a military member."

"Then DNA—or a dentist—is your best bet," Tori surmised.

Osborn nodded.

Tori thought about it. "I suppose this guy could have bought bait from me at one time or another, but I get ten or twenty strangers a week who patronize my shop. If I ever *did* see the guy, he wasn't memorable," she added, trying to be helpful.

Osborn nodded. He looked at her for long seconds before speaking again. "Is it possible Ms. Jackson knew the man?"

"I doubt it. We're pretty close friends. We spend a lot of our downtime together with my roommate, Kathy. If Anissa had a boyfriend, I would've known it."

"And why's that?"

"Have you ever had a best friend, Detective?"

The man looked clueless, and it occurred to Tori that maybe Osborn never had a close friend...he seemed so devoid of personality. Suddenly, she felt sorry for the geeky-looking, middle-aged guy. That said, she didn't want to elaborate. It was bad enough that the three thirty-something women were without male company on a regular basis. But then Tori rethought that scenario. They were three career-minded women. Did they want to be wives and mothers? If the opportunity presented itself, yes. If it didn't...well, they'd talked about it often—over many bottles of wine. The truth was the pickings were pretty slim around these parts. Misogyny seemed to be a universal constant, and a whole TikTok generation of toxic men were out there publishing content that said a woman with her own mind and ambitions was an enemy to be reckoned with. Tori would rather be alone than with the likes of one of those guys. Still, she missed spooning with someone she loved. Then again, the last guy she'd spooned with had dumped her for someone else. On the whole, she'd rather be alone than with someone who wasn't a committed partner.

But all that was neither here nor there.

"Is there anything else you want to ask me, Detective?"

Osborn shook his head. "You may as well shut down your shop and go inside while I talk to Ms. Jackson."

"She had nothing to do with that man's death," Tori said. "I'd stake my life on it."

"Would you really?" Osborn asked her, looking skeptical.

"You bet *your* life I would," Tori said. And she meant it.

∽

ONCE THE BODY had been taken away and the Sheriff's Department cruisers had left the compound, Tori and Anissa retreated to the property's bungalow where they found Kathy had set out sandwiches, along with stemmed glasses and a bottle of chilled white wine waiting to be poured.

"Are you guys okay?" Kathy asked, pushing the plate of tuna salad wedges on white bread and curried deviled eggs toward them. Kathy's solution to life's problems was to feed those in dire straits.

"I'm okay," Tori said with a sigh.

"I wish I felt that good," Anissa said and picked up one of the tuna triangles. She bit into it, closed her eyes, and sighed. "Tunafish sandwiches are one of my favorite comfort foods."

"I wish they were on croissants," Tori said, "but this is almost as good," she quickly added, not wanting to sound ungrateful.

"Sorry. Crappy white bread is all I had to work with," Kathy said.

"Sorry, Kath," Tori apologized. "I'm just feeling a little unsettled."

"You're allowed," Kathy said. "But just this once." It was a lie, and they all knew it.

The three women ate in silence and it wasn't until Kathy refilled their glasses that she spoke. "What happens next?"

"You mean with the dead guy?" Tori asked.

Kathy nodded.

"I hope like hell they don't arrest me for murder," Anissa said and gulped her wine.

"Did you kill him?" Kathy asked.

"No!"

"Then you've got nothing to worry about."

"Says the little white gal," Anissa said and drained her glass.

Tori lifted her glass and swirled the contents. "I think someone dumped the body in the slip farthest from the shop.

"Did they know a storm was on the way, or did they know Anissa didn't take her boat out very often?" The women looked at each other before Tori spoke again. "Whoever killed the guy—or at least wanted to hide the fact that he died, possibly accidentally—wanted to delay the body being found."

Anissa scrutinized her friend's face. "My goodness. Aren't you channeling Miss Marple?"

"You know about those books?" Tori asked.

"Do you think I just got dropped off a turnip truck?" Anissa asked, aghast. "Growing up, my TV got the same PBS channel as yours."

"I didn't mean—" Tori began.

Anissa held up a hand to quiet her. "I know you didn't. I'm just feeling ornery. Cut me a little slack, willya?"

"All the slack you need," Tori said sincerely.

The women polished off the last of the sandwich triangles. "What we need is a decadent dessert," Kathy said.

"And do you have one?" Anissa asked.

"No, but The Bay Bar has peanut butter mud pie on their menu. Why don't I treat the three of us to a slice of it?"

"Sounds like a plan to me," Tori agreed.

Anissa didn't look as convinced. "I don't know," she said, sounding just a little cowed. "A black woman in a redneck bar is just a little—"

"Oh, hush up," Tori said.

"I can always get three slices as take-out," Kathy said.

"You know Noreen and Paul are in your corner," Tori said.

A reluctant Anissa nodded. Like her father, she'd done work for the couple, not only in their bar but remodeling rooms over the bar for rental income.

"I'm sorry. But you know how these things go."

Tori and Kathy shared a knowing look. They sure did.

"I think we need to go on the assumption that Detective Osborn will do his job and find out what happened to that poor man," Kathy said.

"I agree."

Anissa didn't seem so sure. She reached for the wine bottle and refilled her glass.

The silence lengthened among them. It was Kathy who finally spoke. "So, tomorrow is another day. What're we all doing?"

"I'm going to sit in the bait shop and make more pendants," Tori declared.

"And I'm going to say good-bye to my guests and start cleaning," Kathy said with a weary sigh.

The two of them looked at Anissa.

"And I'm going to hope like hell that my life isn't going to be ruined because somebody dumped a body in my little boat."

The silence that followed that statement lengthened until Tori asked, "More wine, anyone?"

CHAPTER 2

Tori was up early the following morning, having had dreams featuring fatal burns, but otherwise made no sense. She tiptoed from her bedroom into the small office she and Kathy shared that had once been her father's bedroom.

Tori powered up her computer, looked at her spreadsheet of monthly expenses, and winced. Yes, she'd had a pretty good season—much better than the year before. She'd rented more boat slips, she'd sold more bait, and even made a modest profit on her fledgling broken-china jewelry sales, but the costs for the renovation—or should that be reclamation—had erased those gains of her boathouse conversion. When finished, she could charge top bucks for the high-end rental. But the tourist season was over, and she probably wouldn't be able to rent that space until May of next year. And she was still undecided if she should outsource the apartment to a management company. She might have to do that, too, when the much more affordable Lotus Lodge reopened. Anissa had brought the old motel building up to code with the water and electrics, and Tori was determined to have the decorative elements ready for the next summer season. How on earth had her grandmother ever run the operation on her own? She must have been the embodiment of a real Wonder Woman. The idea made Tori laugh out loud. Wonder Woman of the TV show and later movies, was a svelte, sexy babe. Tori's grandmother had been overweight, wore glasses, and was rather short but, along with being a force to be reckoned with, she had the kindest heart.

Tori's gaze returned to the columns of numbers on her spreadsheet. It was with sadness that she realized she would have to endure another winter of substitute teaching in the Ward County School District. That realization brought her to the brink of tears.

Tori chewed the first knuckle of her left hand, feeling downhearted. How starry-eyed she'd been when she was in college. How optimistic she'd been at the idea of challenging young people in the pursuit of knowledge. But the truth was kids today weren't interested in learning, and far too many parents weren't invested in their children's education, either.

As a substitute teacher, Tori wasn't in a position to do much more than keep violence from breaking out in her high school classes. That hadn't been her career plan—neither was owning Cannon's Bait & Tackle. Still, she preferred selling bait and renting boats to summer people, lamenting the cost her parents had paid to ship her off to college. Then again...she wasn't exactly on the best terms with her folks, who'd seemed only too happy to send her out of state to college. It was her paternal grandparents who'd thought of her as a shining star. And it was her paternal grandfather who'd given her the deed to the Cannon Compound, including its boat slips, boathouse, bait shop, and family bungalow.

"Wha'cha thinking?" Kathy asked from the doorway, dressed in a rattly old bathrobe and sporting a bad case of bedhead.

"That for all my success this year, I'm still in the hole and will have to substitute teach all winter."

Kathy sat in the chair beside her. Her gaze flickered to the spreadsheet on the computer's monitor. "Yeah, it turns out I was overly optimistic thinking I'd have a lot more bookings at Swans Nest during my first summer season, I ran the numbers the other day and found I only had a forty-five percent occupancy. The weekends were booked but Monday through Thursdays saw only tumbleweeds crossing my yard."

Tori couldn't help but smile at that description, for never had a tumbleweed crossed rural Ward County. She quickly sobered. "What have you got in the way of bookings this fall?"

"A couple of weekends in October and November, but that's all. Let's face it, there's not much to do around here after Labor Day hits."

"Yeah, the lake level drops and, except for a few diehards, most people hauled out their boats weeks ago, calling it quits until Memorial Day rolls around again."

Kathy looked pensive. "Noreen," co-owner with her husband Paul at The Bay Bar and Kathy's next-door neighbor, "is looking for a weekend server. She offered me the job."

"Oh, Kathy...you aren't actually thinking of taking it, are you?" Tori cried.

"If we can work out the timing, yeah, I am."

Tori had supported them the previous winter...but that was before Kathy had a set amount of bills, like utilities for her bed and breakfast, to pay on a monthly basis.

It went without saying that Tori's student teaching a few days a week would support them during this lean time, too. She didn't mind because Kathy pulled her weight by keeping on top of things like cleaning, laundry, and food prep. Those things might have to take a backseat if she was forced to wait tables for twenty or more hours a week for the foreseeable future.

What was she thinking? Kathy didn't sound at all excited at the prospect of being a server and Tori was pretty sure she'd have stuck to the former arrangement if it were fiscally possible.

Tori let out a breath and forced a smile. "Next year we'll be on top of the world," she predicted and even managed to sound optimistic.

"From your lips to God's ears," Kathy agreed. "Hey, I've got some frozen corn muffins I can nuke for breakfast. Want me to fix you one, or do you want to keep working in here?"

Tori stared at her cup of by-now cold tea. "I've studied these numbers long enough. I'm more than ready to get away from them and eat something." She picked up her cup and followed Kathy to the bungalow's shabby kitchen. Tori had hoped by now that she could have revamped the space and figured that any day when one of the ancient major appliances hadn't yet died was sure to be good.

Good as her word, Kathy retrieved the muffins from the freezer and gave them a blast in the microwave. She plopped a plate of muffins on the table and offered to nuke Tori's cup of tea, too, which she accepted. Kathy had made a small bowl of honey butter, which the best friends slathered on their muffins.

No sooner had they taken a bite than they heard a knock at the door. Tori got up to answer it, opening the door so Anissa could enter.

"Good morning, ladies."

"Is it?" Tori asked.

Anissa frowned, studying her friends' faces. "Probably not."

"Sit down and have a cup of coffee and a corn muffin," Kathy said, getting up to grab a cup and pour the coffee while Anissa took her usual seat at the table.

"You ladies look as grim as I feel," Anissa said.

"We've been going over the numbers for our businesses," Tori remarked.

"Yeah, and they aren't good," Kathy added.

Anissa looked just a little guilty, and it was then that Tori noticed an envelope poking out of the bib of Anissa's overalls.

"Is that what I think it is?" she asked.

Anissa lowered her gaze to the tabletop. "Yeah. It's a bill for my most recent services."

Tori held out her hand, and Anissa sheepishly forked over the envelope.

The flap had only been tucked inside, and Tori opened it with ease, unfolding the itemized bill and scrutinizing it.

"I'm sorry," Anissa said contritely, "but I've got to pay my Visa bill for the materials I purchased for the job."

While her grandfather was willing to pay for everything when it came to revitalizing the Lotus Lodge, it was understood that paying for the boathouse conversion project was totally up to Tori.

As she looked at each item, Tori realized that Anissa had no way overcharged her. In fact, she always charged Tori and Kathy far less than the average contractor would.

"I'm sorry," Anissa apologized once again.

"Don't be," Tori assured her. She could pay the bill. She would just have to tighten her financial belt just a little more. For a while. Maybe until spring when she could rent out the boathouse space. "I can write you a check right now," Tori said and got up from her chair.

"Any time in the next week is okay," Anissa assured her, but Tori knew that most people had to pay their bills on or before the first of the month, and October was only days away.

"I'll give it to you before you leave."

"Thanks," Anissa said, her voice small. She was probably in the same financial straits as Tori and Kathy.

"Have you heard from Detective Osborn?" Tori asked Anissa.

She shook her head. "Not a word. Of course, you know my fingerprints are all over my boat."

"Yes, but let's hope they found someone else's as well," Kathy said as a counterpoint.

"I can only hope," Anissa said, without conviction.

"Why don't we all cheer up," Kathy said, slathering a little more honey on her corn muffin and taking a bite.

"So, what's everyone up to today?" Tori asked, trying to sound more cheerful than she felt.

"I've got a job updating a bathroom in Warton," Anissa began. "It might take only a day, but I've booked myself five—just in case. I'll get back to the boathouse as soon as I can."

"There's no hurry," Tori deadpanned. "I can't rent it out until next year anyway."

Anissa's gaze dropped to the remains of the muffin before her.

Tori backpedaled, realizing how her words might have been interpreted. "That wasn't a complaint," she hurriedly explained. "The stars just didn't align."

They sure hadn't.

Anissa looked in Kathy's direction. "And what are you up to?"

Kathy let out a sorrowful sigh. "I may start my new job as a waitress at The Bay Bar tonight or tomorrow."

Anissa's eyes widened. "No!"

"Yeah," Kathy said, her voice flat. "Noreen offered me the job and if I'm going to keep my head above water this winter, I have to bite the bullet and take it, and hope bikers leave good tips."

"Wow," Anissa breathed.

"Yeah," Kathy agreed, sounding totally dejected.

"And I've got another winter of substitute teaching ahead of me," Tori added.

"Wow," Anissa said again. "It sounds like I'm the lucky one. At least I love what I do."

Tori and Kathy nodded in agreement.

"But we're doing what we've got to do to keep our dreams alive," Kathy said, ever the optimist.

"Yeah," Tori agreed. To keep her dream alive, she had better contact the Warton School District and remind them that she was available. She'd do that right after their coffee klatch ended.

Forcing a smile, she said, "Next season, we're all going to see an uptick in our professional lives. All of us."

Kathy raised her cup of coffee. "Cheers to that."

"I'll second that," Anissa said.

Tori raised her mug, too. Now if she could only believe her own prediction.

~

AFTER CONTACTING the Ward Central School district, a heavy-hearted Tori exited the bungalow. The compound's parking lot was empty, so there was no point in opening the bait shop—at least not then. The storm the day before had left the yard cluttered with downed branches and leaves. She was content to let the leaves stay—at least until the next time the grass was cut, but she needed to get those branches picked up so the grass *could* be cut without damage to the tractor or the operator.

Tori hauled out one of the metal trash cans from the storage area behind the bait stop, donned a pair of gardening gloves, and started the tedious task of picking up the debris. She should have worn ear pods to distract her from the chore, but felt too lazy to go back inside and get them. Besides, she had so much mental clutter filling her brain that she found the sounds of life on the bay more soothing. Waves crashed against the breakwall; the wind blew through the trees, and the sound of honking geese flying overhead, who would winter over, was like a balm for her soul.

She'd finished tidying half the yard, and the bin was stuffed with branches and twigs when she saw a figure approach the compound from the edge of the Bay Bridge.

"Hey, Tori."

Tori straightened. It took a few seconds for her to recognize the man. "Is that you, Eric?"

"Nobody but."

Tori had known Eric Mooney for most of her life. He was one of the kids who'd grown up along Resort Road. Although a couple of years younger than Tori's cousin Amber, the two had been best buddies for a few summers. Tori straightened, catching sight of the plastic bucket Eric held in one hand and the fishing pole in the other. "Been fishing?"

"As always," Eric replied good-naturedly.

Tori shook her head. The fishing was good on Lotus Bay. That said, the fish in the bay weren't that good for human consumption—at least not in quantity. For too many years, chemical plants polluted the lake with toxic substances. Tori—and most of her customers—fished for sport and let their catch go. Eric was the only local Tori knew who seemed to subsist on lake fish. After his father's death, he had inherited the house on Resort Road, a summer home that had been converted to year-round living—but not the money for its upkeep. It wasn't long before the place started falling apart. It was now the biggest eyesore on that road filled with new, spectacular homes and seriously upgraded cottages.

"How's things?" Tori asked.

Eric shrugged. "Same old, same old."

Eric never was a great conversationalist.

"How about you? Need any help around here?"

"Are you looking for work?" Tori asked.

Eric shrugged. "I might be."

Tori shook her head. "Sorry, I've got nothing. In fact, I'll have to work a day job through the winter to keep this place afloat next season."

"Oh, yeah? I thought you were about to start making big bucks on your boat house rental."

Tori threw a look over her shoulder. "Yeah, well, that boat has sailed—at least for this season. I can't rent it out until next spring."

"And by then, the Lotus Lodge will open, too. You'll be rolling in dough."

"Yeah, well, It's a long time until summer. Until then, I'm hanging on by a thread."

"Sorry to hear that. But if you hear of anyone needing a day jobber—I'm the guy."

"I'll keep that in mind." Knowing Eric might not have anything else to go with his catch for dinner, Tori thought about her garden. "Hey, I've still got an abundance of tomatoes. Could you use a few?"

Eric shrugged. "I wouldn't say no."

"Great." Tori abandoned her sticks and led Eric to the garden. Since the weather hadn't yet turned, there was still a load of green, ripe, and ready to ripen on a kitchen window sill tomatoes of three varieties. Eric accepted everything she offered, including the green ones, which he said he'd fry coated with cornmeal. Tori found a bag and packed it nearly full.

"There you go."

"Thanks," Eric said, and he did sound grateful. Eating nothing but fish had to get monotonous.

Eric hefted the bag. "Heard you guys had some trouble here last night."

"Yeah," Tori said, but she wasn't up to discussing what she and Anissa had found and seen.

When she didn't elaborate, Eric juggled the bucket, bag of tomatoes, and his fishing pole. "Well, I've already wasted enough of your time. I'd better get going. See ya. And thanks."

"You're welcome—any time," Tori said and watched as Eric crossed the lawn and parking lot, heading north up Resort Road. She liked the guy but always thought he lacked a sense of purpose, which seemed to have increased after the pandemic. Then again, a lot of people had reevaluated their priorities after that awful time—including herself.

With a sigh, Tori donned her gardening gloves once more and went back to tidying the yard. If nothing else, she could offer the sticks to Anissa as kindling for her fireplace—or save them for a bonfire next summer. Her grandparents had hosted them for guests and their kids who stayed at the Lotus Lodge, providing marshmallows for toasting. She remembered those times with fondness. It was another reason families kept coming back year after year ... until the kids got too old to appreciate such simple pleasures.

Don't be such a pessimist, Tori chided herself. She turned her thoughts to the upcoming summer which, considering fall had only just arrived, was a long way off. She also considered obtaining furnishings for her rental properties—not harping on where she'd find the money to pay for them, but how much she'd enjoy decorating the spaces.

It was better than thinking about the present.

CHAPTER 3

Shoulders slumped, Kathy closed the bungalow's door behind her and headed toward The Bay Bar. It was only a hundred yards or so from the Cannon Compound, but it felt like miles as she slogged along on that gray early evening. A couple of cars were usually parked in the lot—guys getting a beer on the way home—but at that time, the lot was empty save for Noreen's and Paul's cars.

Kathy opened the door and entered, somewhat cheered by the neon signs and the blast of warm air that greeted her. Neither Paul nor Noreen was in evidence, and the only sounds came from one of the TVs airing a round-up for the weekend football games.

"Hello!" Kathy called.

"Coming," came Noreen's voice from behind the swinging door to the kitchen. Seconds later, she entered the restaurant. "Welcome to the bar! Are you ready to start your new career?"

Career? Gosh, she sure hoped not. "Ready as I'll ever be," Kathy said with forced cheer.

Noreen moved behind the bar and rummaged around for a few seconds before coming up with a folded shirt. The wait staff at The Bay Bar had no real uniform—just a T-shirt with the bar's logo and dark slacks, which Kathy had donned before leaving home.

Noreen handed her a shirt that was miles too big for Kathy. "Sorry. But that's all I've got at the moment," she apologized. "I'm going to put in a new order soon." But she didn't say *how* soon.

"No problem," Kathy said, putting on a smile.

"Check out the chalkboard. That's where you'll find our special of the day," Noreen said, handing Kathy an order pad. Kathy was supposed to be one of two servers on that shift, "but Brittany called in sick, and Diane can't come in to cover for her until eight," Noreen began. "So…you're going to have to go solo for the first couple of hours," she said, her voice going softer with each word.

Kathy blinked. "Solo as in…no training?"

"Well, you've been around the bar a lot. You know our routine."

Not really.

"Paul will be behind the bar. If you have any questions, he can help out. And don't be afraid to ask him anything."

Like where the napkins were stored, or the cutlery, or how to operate the coffeemaker.

"Thanks," Kathy deadpanned.

"Not a problem. I've got more prep in the kitchen," Noreen said, gave Kathy a smile, and disappeared behind the swinging door.

Kathy stood near the bar, rehearsing the night's specials from the chalkboard on the wall. Soup: Clam chowder. Appetizer: Clams casino. Entree: Fried haddock with French fries, coleslaw, tartar sauce and lemon. Desserts: Push the strawberry cheesecake that was getting close to its use-by date.

She was ready.

A couple entered the bar. The guy was dressed in biker leathers and a blue bandanna, and the woman wore jeans and a leather coat. Both had to be twenty years older than Kathy. She picked up a couple of menus and stepped forward to greet them.

"Hi! I'm Kathy. Let me show you to your table."

"We'll sit where we want," the man said gruffly.

"Uh, well…okay," Kathy said, and timidly followed the duo to the prime seats in front of the bar that overlooked the bay.

"I'm sorry, sir, but that table is reserved."

The burly man grabbed the placard, slapped it on an adjacent table, pivoted, and leaned close to Kathy's face. "Are you gonna stop us from sitting here?"

Kathy was about to reply when she heard someone clear his throat behind her.

"Hey, Eddie—Pearl. Don't tell me you didn't see the reserved sign on that table," Paul said, sounding quite jovial. "Why don't you folks take that table right next to it? Just park yourselves there, and I'll give you a free round of Genesee."

Eddie leveled a blistering glare at Kathy. "I guess we could sit there," he agreed.

"Kath, why don't you tell these fine folks the specials and then come get their drinks."

"Thanks, Paul," Kathy said gratefully.

Paul slapped Eddie on the back in a friendly gesture and headed toward the bar. Kathy replaced the reserved sign on the center table before handing the man and woman their menus. Eddie tossed it back at Kathy, and it fell to the floor. "I don't need no stinkin' menu. I came for the fish fry."

Kathy recovered the menu. "And you ma'am?"

"Ma'am? I ain't no ma'am," the woman snapped. She'd long since passed the designation of Miss. "I wanna think about it. Get our drinks and I'll let you know what I want."

Kathy forced a smile. "Sure thing." She left the table, feeling the heat of the couple's ill-will blistering her back.

Paul poured the beers from the tap as Kathy approached the bar.

"Sorry, Kath, but you've pulled two of our most obnoxious regulars as your first table."

"How bad are they likely to be?" she asked timidly.

"Nothing is gonna satisfy them. But if they give you a hard time, let me know. I've been looking for an excuse to ban them from the bar."

His words made Kathy feel even more uncomfortable.

Paul shoved the Pilsner glasses toward Kathy. She picked them up and headed to greet her difficult patrons again, setting the glasses before them.

"What? No cocktail napkins?" Pearl snapped.

"Oh, I'm sorry. This is my first shift here at The Bay Bar," Kathy said and laughed nervously. "I'll get you some."

"Don't bother," the man said, grabbed his glass, and downed at least a third of the beer in one gulp.

"Well, I want one," Pearl growled, giving Kathy a sour look.

Kathy mustered a smile. "Coming right up." She retrieved said napkin and returned to the table. She set the napkin in front of the woman, who plunked her glass onto the surface and not on the napkin as though in a show of defiance.

"Are you ready to order?" Kathy asked with a false bravado.

"I told you. I want a fish fry," Eddie growled.

"Make that two," the woman said.

Kathy dutifully wrote down their orders. "Two fish fries coming right up."

"And don't let 'em sit under the heat lamp. We want them *hot* from the fryer," Tommy declared.

"Yes, sir," Kathy said.

Kathy headed for the kitchen to hand in the order.

"Here you go," she told Noreen, who was already drenched in sweat behind the grill. "First order of the night. It's for a disagreeable couple called Eddie and Pearl."

"Oh, not them again," Noreen groaned. "All they do is

complain. They hate everything. We're seriously thinking of asking them to never darken our door again."

"So Paul said."

"Don't you let them intimidate you. I promise you, most of our regulars are real sweethearts."

Kathy fought the urge to dispute that.

When she returned to the dining room, she found another couple waiting to be seated. They were the ones who'd reserved the center table and they couldn't have been nicer. They ordered a bottle of wine and told her it was their anniversary.

"How long have you been married?" Kathy asked the couple, who looked to be in their sixties.

"Thirty-eight wonderful years," the woman said, reaching over to clasp her husband's hand. He smiled.

"Would you like me to bring the wine before you make your dinner decisions?" Kathy asked.

"Yeah, and then we'll just look at the menu and let you know."

"Sure thing."

Kathy turned toward Eddie and Pearl, who had guzzled their beers. "Can I get you another round?"

"Only if it's on the house," Eddie growled.

"How about I bring a carafe of water to the table?" Kathy suggested.

"Forget it. Water is so…so tasteless," Pearl muttered, her gaze focused out the window on the clear, pale sky over Lake Ontario.

Kathy heard the ringing of a bell from the kitchen. The fish fries were ready. She hurried off to retrieve them. Eddie wanted his *hot*.

Less than a minute later, she delivered the plates to the table. "Two fish fries," she said, setting plates before the couple."

"What is this?" Eddie yelled.

"Your fish fry," Kathy said.

"I didn't order a fish fry. I ordered a burger—well done. And with onion rings."

"Me, too!" Pearl declared.

Kathy clenched her fists. "No, sir. You and your companion both ordered fish fries. I wrote it down on my pad." She reached into her pocket and withdrew the article, showing them the copy.

"The hell we did," Eddie roared. "And where's our second round of free beers?"

Kathy knew there was no way she was going to please these people, whom both Paul and Noreen had said were difficult. Difficult? They were complete jerks.

Eddie shoved the plate away. "Bring us our burgers—and it had better be damned fast."

Kathy stood there for long seconds, unsure of what she should do. Finally, she picked up the plates and took them back to the kitchen. She set them back on the counter under the heat lamp and swallowed. It was all she could do not to cry.

Noreen turned to look at her. "Those...people...said they didn't order fish fries. They now say they ordered burgers—with onion rings."

Noreen's gaze traveled down to the perfectly fried fish and chips and the lovingly placed piece of parsley that served as a garnish.

For a moment, Kathy was afraid Noreen might explode and berate her, but it turned out her ire wasn't focused on The Bay Bar's newest server.

"Those bastards," she practically spat. "This isn't the first time they've pulled this crap on a new server."

Kathy let out the breath she didn't know she'd been holding.

"What happens now?" she asked.

"I cook two burgers and toss two perfectly fried pieces of fish —unless you think your cats will eat them."

"They'd love it," Kathy said, her voice shaky.

Noreen nodded. "I'll strip off the beer batter and stick the fillets in the fridge for your kitties. And I'll cook those burgers, but you tell Paul to come talk to me. I'm not putting up with the crap those two pull every time they come into our place. I want them banned. Now!"

Noreen might be small in stature, but she was a powerhouse.

Kathy did as she was told and spoke to Paul before she checked on her other patrons, who seemed perfectly nice, ordering the clams casino and strip steaks medium well done.

Eddie snagged Kathy's arm as she passed. "Where's our grub?" he demanded.

Kathy shook off his hand, took a breath to fortify herself, and forced a smile. "Coming right up."

"And where's that water you promised?" Pearl demanded.

Kathy bit her tongue so that she wouldn't blurt that they'd previously rejected her offer to bring it. "I'll get it for you now."

"You do that," Pearl practically spat.

Kathy felt like spitting into the glass carafe as she filled it with ice and cold water. She didn't, of course, but the urge was definitely there.

A couple of guys entered the restaurant but headed straight for the bar, so Kathy continued to the kitchen.

Noreen seemed to be everywhere at once, multitasking. How she did so much on her own was rather astonishing.

"The burgers will be up in another minute or two. I'll ring the bell when they're ready. Go back to the dining room in case any other customers come in."

"Right," Kathy said and left the unbearably hot kitchen. No wonder Noreen kept a svelte figure. She must sweat half her body weight every night stationed near the commercial ovens and grill.

Another couple entered the bar, and Kathy successfully sat them, taking their drink orders before the bell rang in the kitchen. She hurried to retrieve the burger orders and quickly dispatched them to her ornery customers.

"There you go. Burgers and fries," she said cheerfully.

"We didn't order burgers," Eddie thundered. "We ordered fish fries."

Kathy took a breath, fighting the urge to pick up the heavy restaurantware plate and smash it onto the obnoxious man's head. "Sir, I brought you both fish fries. You said you ordered burgers."

"Well, we don't want them," Eddie said, pushing his plate away from his ample belly.

Kathy wasn't about to argue with him. Instead, she pivoted and stalked straight toward the bar.

Paul was waiting for her. "They said they ordered the fish they already refused, right?"

Kathy nodded meekly.

Paul's expression underwent a terrible transformation as he straightened to his full height, then walked around the bar, heading for the dining room. Kathy timidly followed behind him.

When Paul arrived at Eddie's table, he bent down, laying a hand on the man's shoulder and, from Eddie's expression, apparently squeezing it hard.

"Eddie, Pearl," he addressed them, his voice low and menacing. "I'm going to cut you some slack. This. One. Last. Time."

Eddie swung an uncomfortable gaze upon The Bay Bar's proprietor.

"We're going to comp you these burgers. And then you're going to leave the premises and never darken our door again. And if you leave a bad Yelp review, I will make sure you live to regret it. Do I make myself clear?"

"You can't threaten us," Pearl asserted.

"The hell I can't," Paul said, his voice barely above a whisper. "I have the brotherhood of over fifty biker regulars I can sic on you and make your lives a living hell. Do I make myself clear?"

Kathy saw Eddie swallow—twice—before he nodded.

Paul straightened, plastering on as phony a smile as Kathy had ever seen. "Enjoy your meals," he roared, slapping Eddie so hard on the back that the man's head nearly smacked the table.

Neither Eddie nor Pearl commented.

As Paul strode away, Kathy braved a smile. "Can I get you some ketchup for those burgers?"

∽

IT WAS after eleven when Tori heard the bungalow's back door open and close. "I'm in the living room," she called.

Kathy practically slunk into the room, and Tori caught a whiff of stale cooking odors. "Hey, how'd things go?" she asked brightly, but she could tell by her roommate's slumped shoulders and the set to her mouth that Kathy was about to burst into tears.

"Sit down? Do you want a cup of tea or something?"

Kathy flopped onto the ratty couch that Tori's grandparents had probably bought two or three decades before. "Something a helluva lot stronger than tea."

"It was that bad?" Tori ventured.

Kathy sighed, and a tear leaked from her left eye. "You wouldn't believe it if I told you."

Tori jumped up, raced to the kitchen, grabbed and opened the bottle of asti spumante from the fridge they'd been saving for a special occasion. She poured glasses for both of them before returning to the living room.

"Thanks," Kathy said gratefully and nearly downed the whole glass. "Noreen sent some fish home for Daisy and the boys."

"At least the cats will be overjoyed come breakfast time," Tori said. She softened her tone. "It wasn't *all* terrible...was it?"

"No. There were some really nice people, and I got some really good tips. She dug into the pocket of her slacks and brought out a wad of cash—mostly ones—and some change. Still, her expression wasn't triumphant.

"What are you going to do with your tips?" Tori asked.

"Put them in a jar. And after a few days, head to the bank...I guess."

"Were Paul and Noreen happy with your work?"

"Yeah, but I think they were relieved when Diane, one of their regular servers, came in for the late shift. She, at least, knew what she was doing."

Tori studied her friend's downhearted expression. "Are you going to quit?"

"I can't afford to. But I'm grateful that they'll let me choose my own hours. Until I can make Swans Nest pay for itself, I'll have to keep waitressing."

The women sipped their drinks. When the glasses emptied, Tori refilled them.

"Okay, so we both hate our second jobs," Tori said at last. "But it can't last forever. Just through the winter—so we can get through the lull in trade from our regular jobs as entrepreneurs."

"Six or more months of this seems like an eternity to me right now."

"Facing all those unfamiliar students and trying to keep peace in the classrooms feels the same to me," Tori said.

"You're right," Kathy agreed. "I'm sorry I dumped my crap on you. I'd rather work as a server with Paul looking after me than face a room full of potentially unruly teenagers."

"There's a reason I wear glasses to school instead of contacts," Tori said. "They command at least some semblance of respect."

Kathy took another big swig of her wine. "I'm probably being overly dramatic. Most of the people I waited on tonight were nice. Some of them tipped really well," Kathy reiterated, close to tears.

"And the others?" Tori asked.

Kathy shrugged. "There's not much else in the way of work for me around here," she said, plucking at the oversized T-shirt. "And I only have to cross the road to get to the bar. And I didn't have to buy a uniform." She gazed into her wineglass. "I can do this. At least for the winter. I just hope I won't have to do it every off season. That would just kill me."

"Me, too," Tori agreed, thinking about another year of substitute teaching, and raised her glass.

As for the future, they just had to wait and see.

CHAPTER 4

It had been more than a day since Tori had spoken to anyone from the Ward County Sheriff's Department. She wasn't sure if that was a good or bad thing. She'd learned from listening to the morning news that not only were the skies to continue their gray hue but that the man she and Anissa had found two days before was one Charles Stanton, an employee of the local power company. Well, that made sense. Playing around with high-tension wires could be—and in this case, definitely was—fatal. Being dumped after death didn't fit the profile of an accident.

After making her usual pot of tea, Tori retreated to the office and fired up her computer.

Tori checked the online obituaries, looking for news of one Charles "Chuck" Stanton. The funeral home had posted it on their website, and perhaps the man's family would pay for a death notice in the Rochester Sunday paper. Usually, such announcements mirrored what was on the funeral home's site. Still, Tori decided she'd look the next morning.

Tori scanned the home's brief obit. Charles "Chuck" Stanton, predeceased by his parents Ernest and Jane Stanton, and brother

Lawrence. Survived by his wife of 26 years Alice, and the sunshine of his life, his chocolate lab Daisy.

Tori felt a pang of grief for the woman and the now masterless pooch. Her beloved cat was named Daisy, and the name gave Tori a small bridge of connection with the poor, unfortunate man.

Tori read on about the plans for interment and that the family had designated that in lieu of flowers, donations should be sent to the Ward County Humane Society. Tori would make sure she sent something to the charity as her cat Daisy, and Kathy's boys Henry and Larry, had all been rescues.

Her stomach growled, and Tori decided it was time for breakfast.

Once in the kitchen, Tori warmed her tea in the microwave and checked the freezer to see what leftovers Kathy had brought over from Swans Nest. A slice of Quiche Lorraine would hit the spot, and she took it out to thaw before she opened the bungalow's door to retrieve the paper edition of the Democrat & Chronicle—Rochester's local rag—from the bungalow's front step and went back into the warm kitchen. Her grandfather had paid for a two-year subscription a couple of months before he'd decided to relocate to Florida with his new love. Old-fashioned as it was, Tori liked to read what little local news, the comics it contained, and the advice columnist. Reading about other people's problems always seemed to put her own into their proper perspective. She got no reprieve on that day.

Autumn Saturdays were hit or miss. If the weather was good, some brave souls might show up and rent a boat, buy some bait, and spend a few hours out on the bay, and with nothing else to do, Tori knew she had to open the bait shop—just in case. Kathy would probably spend the day working at Swans Nest, cleaning, decorating, or baking, and then she had her shift at The Bay Bar in the evening. Anissa had that bathroom to work on in Warton, and if she was tired, she wasn't likely to show up in the evening. That meant Tori would be alone most of the day and all evening.

Sometimes life just sucked.

∼

THE BAY BAR was devoid of customers when Kathy arrived for her second shift fifteen minutes before her starting time. Paul was behind the bar, cutting fruit garnishes, as a baseball game played on one of the big-screen TVs across the dining room. "Hey, Kath. Take a gander at tonight's specials, willya?"

"Sure thing," Kathy said and paused to hang up her jacket. She glanced at the board; she'd seen the same things listed on many a Saturday night when she, Tori, and/or Anissa would stop in for dessert or a drink at the bar.

"Honey!" came Noreen's voice from the kitchen. "Can you bring me a ginger ale?"

"I can take it to her," Kathy volunteered.

Paul pivoted to fill a plastic tumbler with ice and squirt the soda from the well dispenser. "Here ya go," he said, shoving the glass in Kathy's direction. She headed toward the swinging door that separated the kitchen from the dining room.

"One glass of ginger ale coming up," Kathy called.

Noreen was in the process of scraping the top of the grill with a metal spatula, when suddenly she tossed it onto the greasy surface in frustration.

"What's wrong?" Kathy asked, handing Noreen the tumbler.

"Oh, Jimmy," the busboy, "quit this morning. He said he could make more money working for Q&R Trash picking up garbage than he could here."

Kathy didn't doubt it.

"He hasn't been all that reliable, but I'm sorry, you're going to have to bus your tables again tonight and maybe every night until —or unless—we can find someone to take Jimmy's place."

Kathy had enough to take care of without cleaning and sanitizing tables. But she did have an idea for a possible solution to the problem. "Do you know Eric Mooney?"

Noreen frowned. "I've heard of him. Lives in a shack up on Resort Road."

"That's the one. He told Tori he wants to work but no one will hire him."

Noreen's gaze narrowed. "And why's that? Is he a druggie?"

"Not that I know of."

"Is he lazy?"

"I didn't think so. He fishes to keep himself in food—"

"He's eating the bottom feeders here on the bay? That's not a good choice."

"When you're hungry, you make do," Kathy said sympathetically.

Noreen didn't look convinced.

"Could you at least give him a chance?"

"How do you even know he'd be interested in the job?"

"All I have to do is ask him," Kathy remarked.

"When?"

"Tomorrow."

"Well, if he says yes—he's hired. On a trial basis," Noreen emphasized.

"Absolutely," Kathy affirmed.

"Okay, then," Nora retrieved her spatula and turned her attention back to scraping the grill. "If he's interested. He can start tomorrow night."

"And the pay?" Kathy asked.

Noreen gave her the bad news. Restaurant workers really were screwed. Still, Eric said he wanted a job. How bad would it look for Kathy if he declined the offer?

Kathy guessed she'd just have to find out.

"Of course, you know you're supposed to tip out," Noreen said.

"Tip out?" Kathy asked, confused.

"Yeah, share a portion of your tips with the busboys."

Kathy frowned. She was making far below minimum wage as a server. It was the tips that made the job worthwhile. "How much?"

"Fifteen percent. Are you okay with that?"

"Well…." No, she wasn't. But if that was what was expected. "I guess."

Noreen nodded. "Good. Now, I've got a question for you. Have you got anything on tap next weekend?"

"Just working here."

"Great. Because I was thinking I might be able to steer a little something *your* way."

"What do you mean?"

"Nothing much. My sister-in-law is looking for a wedding shower venue for a small group of friends and family. It's very last minute."

Kathy inwardly cringed. Working with friends and family often caused hard feelings. "What did you have in mind?" Kathy asked. Hosting a bridal party meant a lot of cleaning, baking, and then the cleanup afterward. "I thought you hosted parties at the bar."

"My sister-in-law doesn't want her shower to be in a *biker* bar," Noreen said. "She wants something fancier. Swans Nest should fit the bill."

"Well, it is short notice, but I guess I could—"

"*I'll* be catering the party," Noreen volunteered. "We just need a place to host it."

"I guess…" Kathy said lamely.

"Great," Noreen said cheerfully. "Could you offer me the friends and family discount?"

"I … I never really thought about renting out the parlor for a party that I didn't cater myself."

"We're on a pretty tight budget," Noreen pressed.

This conversation was getting awkward. "A hundred," Kathy said.

Noreen frowned but said nothing.

"Seventy-five?" Kathy tried again.

Noreen looked away.

"Fifty," Kathy said firmly, declining to add that it was her last offer.

Noreen seemed to mull over the offer. "I'll give you a tentative yes. I need to talk to Barb and can get back to you tomorrow."

Kathy forced a smile. "Great."

"Kathy!" Paul called.

"Customers," Noreen said flatly, and took another slug of her ginger ale. "Saturday, we're usually hit with a lot of prime rib and steak orders—push the stuffed pork chops, as we're overstocked."

"Sure thing," Kathy said and hurried into the dining room to meet the evening's first guests. She could see through the window in the door that a couple of other cars were pulling into the lot.

It was going to be another busy night at The Bay Bar.

CHAPTER 5

The sun hadn't yet hit the horizon, and Tori hadn't closed the bait shop, waiting for her last boat to be turned in. Her grand total for the day was 60 bucks. Well, that was more than she'd made the day before. She could buy groceries with that—at least enough for a few days—and maybe a couple of bottles of cheap wine. But with the lengthening shadows came a chill. Taking up her binoculars, she looked across the water. No sign of her boat. That gave her time to run into the bungalow and get something warmer to wear.

She and Kathy had made a pact not to turn on the heat until at least October first, which was still days away. Instead, she headed for her bedroom to grab her favorite sweater. Kathy had begged her countless times to ditch the light blue cardigan, not only because it was miles too big for Tori but also because Tori had replaced the missing buttons with whatever she could find. It had belonged to Tori's grandmother, Josie, and therefore held a special place in her heart.

After donning it, she turned to draw the curtains and glanced out her bedroom window to see a lone, silhouetted figure standing on the dock. She'd only been gone a couple of minutes and hadn't heard a car pull into the lot. The woman's shoulder-length, graying hair blew in the wind. Clearly, she hadn't arrived at the compound to fish or buy bait. Usually, Tori ignored the strangers who came and went, but for some reason, she felt she needed to speak to the woman.

Tori hurried out the door, crossing her arms over her chest to ward off the chill. "Hello!"

The woman turned, and it was apparent by her facial expression that she was in deep distress.

"Would you like a cup of coffee? It's complimentary," Tori offered, glad she hadn't turned off the shop's coffeemaker.

The woman's head turned back toward the bay for long seconds, then she turned, and walked toward the bait shop.

Tori waited and held the door open to allow the woman to enter the shop's relative warmth before she retreated behind the sale's counter. "How do you like your brew?"

"Black, with just a little sugar," the woman said.

Tori turned toward the pot she kept going for herself and a few of the regulars. She poured the steaming liquid into a paper cup, adding half a teaspoon of sugar, stirred, and handed it to the woman.

"Thanks."

"You're welcome. My name's Tori. I own the shop and the property. And you are?"

"Alice Stanton."

Tori hitched in a breath. The surname of the man she and Anissa had found was the same.

"My husband—" Alice began.

"I know," Tori interrupted, hoping to make what the woman had to say land just a bit easier.

Alice stared at her. "You found my Chuck?"

Tori nodded. Had Alice seen the burns on her husband's hands, or had she been spared that?

"I never met your husband. He wasn't one of my regular customers."

Alice shook her head. "I'm pretty sure he patronized your competition. That's why it was so strange that he was found in one of your boats...." Her voice trailed off.

"I'm so sorry for your loss," Tori said with sincerity. "How long were you married?"

"Nearly twenty-seven years. Chuck was always good with money. We both worked. We weren't lucky enough to have children, so we were able to build up a pretty hefty retirement fund. He didn't *have* to keep working for the power company. He—" But then she didn't continue; instead, taking a fortifying gulp of coffee. She shook her head, chewed her lip, and looked about to cry.

"I asked him to retire. I *begged* him! He could have had a job as a bus driver. He loved kids! He wouldn't have had to work a lot of hours. He'd have had summers off! I *told* him!" the woman said shrilly and then collapsed to her knees, sobbing so hard her whole body shook. "We were supposed to grow old together. What am I going to do without him?" she wailed.

Fighting tears, Tori hurried around the counter, crouched, and rested a hand on the woman's shoulder. Alice turned to clutch Tori, crying so hard Tori was afraid the woman might have a seizure. Tori held onto her. "I'm so sorry. I'm so, so sorry," she crooned and patted the woman's back.

Still, a long minute or two passed before Alice's sobs began to subside. Tori had no doubt this wasn't the first in a long parade of tears the woman would experience.

∾

AFTER HER ENCOUNTER with Alice Stanton, Tori was feeling pretty down when she got a text from Anissa. *I'm bored!*

I'm saved! Tori thought.

Come on down to my place, and we can be bored together, Tori answered.

Ten minutes later, Anissa's truck pulled up outside the bungalow. Tori decided she wasn't up to talking about Alice more than once that evening and resolved not to mention it until Kathy returned later that evening. Anissa entered the house just as the air popper finished, and Tori poured melted butter over the top of a mound of fluffy kernels.

"Popcorn!" Anissa cried. "One of my favorite foods." She shrugged out of her jacket and placed it on the back of her usual chair.

"Well, we gotta eat," Tori said, sprinkled a generous amount of salt over the snack, then she tore a couple of sheets from the roll of paper towels, and placed them and the bowl on the table.

"We should do something other than just eat," Anissa suggested.

"I'm saving the wine until Kathy comes home from The Bay Bar. After her first shift, she really needed it."

"That bad?"

"She had a couple of difficult customers."

Anissa didn't look surprised. "Well, we need to do *something*."

"I've got a load of board games. We could play Uno."

Anissa wrinkled her nose. "I don't really like card games."

"Chess?"

Anissa shook her head. "I've had a long day. I don't want to have to think too hard."

"Shoots and Ladders?"

Anissa rolled her eyes.

"Monopoly?" Tori offered in desperation.

Anissa brightened. "James and I used to play that for hours on snowy days."

"No snow—yet," Tori muttered, "but it would sure kill time before Kathy gets home."

"I get to be the car!" Anissa called. They'd played before. Tori had an older version of the game that still harbored the original tokens.

"That's fine with me; I prefer the boot."

They did rock, paper, scissors to see who'd be the banker, with Anissa winning.

The women laughed and stuffed their faces with popcorn. Tori definitely had more property than Anissa when the back door opened and a weary-looking Kathy entered the kitchen.

"'Home again, home again—jiggity jig,'" Tori quoted.

"If only I felt that cheerful," Kathy said and hung up her jacket.

"Another brutal shift?" Anissa guessed.

Kathy shook her head. "No worse than last night."

Tori had already filled Anissa in on that debacle. "Well, I had a jarring experience this afternoon, too."

"What?" Anissa asked, confused.

Tori told them about her encounter with Alice Stanton. "It was awful. The poor woman cried so hard I was afraid for her. She loved her husband *so* much. It almost makes me want to remain single for the rest of my life just so I never have to go through that kind of pain."

"You don't mean that," Kathy admonished her.

"Oh, yes, I do," Tori asserted, her eyes filling with tears. But then she backpedaled. "Well, maybe not." Then again, she hadn't had a relationship—let alone a date—in over two years. Some people were destined to be alone. Maybe she was one of them.

"I'm sorry you had to go through that," Anissa said, "but I can understand why you feel like you do. Remember that song 'Love Hurts?' Boy, does it ever!"

It was abundantly clear that the women were all unlucky in love. Was it them? Were they so unworthy of affection, or had they just fallen into the habit of being attracted to terrible men? There were plenty of good guys out there…they just all seemed to be taken. It all came down to availability. They were three smart women living in an area where intelligence in the so-called *weaker* sex was not appreciated by the overabundance of available men who felt that women weren't considered equals. Or at least...that's what it seemed.

"Please tell me you two had a better day than me," Tori pleaded.

Kathy ducked her head, looking just a little sheepish. "Well, sort of."

"Sort of?" Tori asked.

"This afternoon, I booked a bridal shower."

"That's fantastic," Anissa said, sounding overly enthusiastic.

"Tell us more," Tori said.

"It's for Noreen's sister-in-law, Barb."

"We've never met her," Tori commented.

"Neither have I," Kathy admitted. "She and Noreen are going to talk about it tomorrow."

"Who's she marrying?" Anissa asked.

"According to Paul, someone she met at the bar."

"What else do you know about her?" Anissa asked.

"Seems like she and Paul are close. He said Barb is some kind of aide who works at the health center outside Warton."

Ward County had a hospital with a good reputation, but it was at least twenty-five minutes from the Cannon Compound. The health center was only open during weekday business hours, but they would take in walk-ins who had minor issues—like fish hooks embedded in fingers and even backs, from careless casters.

"How big a party?" Tori asked.

"Medium," Kathy said with what sounded like embarrassment. "Twelve to fifteen people, I guess." Kathy didn't sound all that confident.

"What is it you're *not* saying?" Anissa asked.

Kathy's head dipped even lower. "I gather Noreen's sister-in-law is known to be a little difficult."

"Difficult how?" Anissa pressed.

"Noreen hinted that she looks down her nose at the bar—that it wasn't good enough for her last-minute shower."

Tori wrinkled her nose. "That doesn't make sense. You just said she met the guy *at* the bar?"

Kathy shrugged.

Anissa frowned. "Are you sure you want to deal with Bridezilla?"

Kathy let out a sigh. "Considering my financial status—and how dire it might become during the off-season—I have to take just about every booking that comes my way."

"They aren't going to get married at Swans Nest, right?" Tori asked.

Kathy shook her head. "Paul said they've booked the American Legion hall for that."

"Does that bug you?" Anissa asked.

Kathy shook her head. "Not a bit. By next summer, I'll have a tent and can accommodate a crowd *outside*. Unless the crowd is ten or fifteen people, I don't even want to contemplate pulling off a winter wedding at my inn."

"Well, one day it *could* happen," Tori said hopefully.

"I'll just be glad to book guests around special weekends, like Halloween, Valentine's Day, and Easter."

"Do you need to find an off-season job?" Anissa asked.

"That's why I'm at the bar."

Anissa shook her head. "No, I mean—"

"I've thought about catering," Kathy interrupted her. "I'm not sure how I could advertise it."

"Just letting the locals know you're here is one way. Maybe you should put an ad in the local Penny Saver. And you could put up a poster in Tom's Grocery Store in Warton."

"Yeah. I'll call the local rag to see what their ads cost. Catering *might* just save me."

Tori turned to Anissa. "And how did your day go?"

Anissa's expression soured. "Not so good."

"In what way?" Kathy asked.

"I had another conversation with Detective Osborn, but that wasn't the worst."

"What was?" Kathy asked.

Anissa's gaze dipped to the floor. "My mother."

Oh, dear. Tori and Kathy were well aware that Anissa's mother considered her the family's black sheep. Her brother, James, was successful in the medical field, while Anissa followed her father's lead by going into the building trade. No doubt about it, an oral surgeon made a lot more cash than a handywoman who aspired to be a contractor. Tori had given Anissa that moniker, and she'd shined. Anissa was building a reputation as a go-to gal for people who needed a handywoman and if she couldn't do the job herself—which she could if pushed—she could at least subcontract that work out. Slowly but steadily, she was building that kind of network.

"What's going on?" Tori asked.

Anissa frowned. "I called to wish her happy birthday, but apparently that wasn't enough. James and his family were taking her out to dinner. In contrast, a phone call is just lip service."

"Did your brother invite you to be part of the celebration?" Kathy asked.

"No." Anissa frowned. "James and his wife—who also acts as his receptionist and scheduler—have enough to think about. Michelle probably didn't figure not including me would be a problem. She's a gem and has to bite her tongue nearly as often as me when dealing with my mother."

"Maybe you could take your mom out to lunch or something to calm the waters," Tori suggested.

Anissa shook her head. "Nope. That wouldn't appease her. I've just about given up pleasing that woman. I think the happiest day of my daddy's life was the day she left him. It wasn't mine, of course, but it was a relief for James and me."

"I'm sorry you're going through that," Tori said sincerely.

"From what you've said, you experienced something pretty darn close with your parents," Anissa remarked.

"They're still together, but yeah—nothing I do pleases them, either."

Tori's mother had a career. When Tori arrived, she was considered more of a burden. Once, in a fit of anger, her mother had shouted that Tori had been an unplanned pregnancy. Once heard, those words were never forgotten, and Tori's affection for her mother had waned, until now she thought of the woman as someone she'd just as soon avoid. And her Dad? She felt sorry for him. He always seemed beaten. Then there were Grandma Josie and Gramps, her paternal grandparents, who'd loved her unconditionally. Well, at least Josie had. Gramps loved her, too, but there were parameters around his affection. Or maybe it was just that he was averse to showing mushy affection. He'd had a hard life, and it was only due to his lottery win the year before that he felt secure enough to loosen up.

Kathy crossed the kitchen and opened the fridge, taking out a bottle of Chardonnay she'd acquired earlier that day.

"About time, too," Anissa muttered.

Kathy set the bottle down on the counter, retrieved three small wine glasses, and filled them.

"What are we going to drink to?" Tori asked, accepting one of the glasses.

"To better days?" Anissa suggested.

Kathy hoisted her glass. "They can't come soon enough."

No, Tori thought, they couldn't.

CHAPTER 6

Although Kathy had eaten at The Bay Bar—a perk she appreciated—Tori and Anissa had snacked on only popcorn. Kathy doctored a frozen pizza, and they polished off the bottle of wine before Anissa left for home.

"I'm bushed," Tori said. "I think I'll hit the sack."

"Before you go, I was wondering if you'd take a walk with me tomorrow."

Tori frowned. "Where to?"

"The busboy at the bar quit—I've had to bus my own tables, and it's a pain in the butt when we're as busy as we were tonight. Do you think Eric Mooney would be interested in taking the job?"

"He did sound kind of desperate," Tori remarked.

"So, unless it's raining, will you walk down the road with me tomorrow morning to talk to him?"

Tori shrugged. "Sure thing."

"Good."

The women said their goodnights and retired to their respective bedrooms.

Come morning, Kathy was up first. When Tori arrived in the

kitchen, the fixings for French toast sat on the counter. Kathy poured coffee for herself and tea for Tori.

"What time do you think we should visit Eric?"

Tori glanced at the clock. "I dunno. Maybe ten o'clock? Some people like to sleep in on Sundays."

"Since the guy doesn't have a job, he might sleep 'til noon every day of the week," Kathy commented.

Tori shook her head. "Nah, I see him fishing from the bridge pretty early in the morning. He's probably been up for hours."

"Okay, then right after breakfast, we'll head up the road."

The dew was heavy on the grass as they crossed the compound's gravel parking lot and headed north up Resort Road.

"It always amazes me how much the houses along the road have changed since I was a kid," Tori said, taking in a structure that had to be four- or five-thousand square feet of living space. "Back then, most of the houses were summer cottages. The town must be pulling in big bucks with property taxes on these behemoths."

"You're paying through the nose yourself."

"Yeah," Tori agreed. "It's my biggest expense. It doesn't seem fair that even tiny waterfront properties pay more in property taxes than farms with hundreds—or thousands—of acres of land."

"Yeah," Kathy agreed.

"My grandma once objected to a property tax hike and do you know what the county tax collector told her? 'Then just sell off. Someone else will be glad to have your property and pay for it.'" Tori shook her head. "If my grandma had been into voodoo, I'm sure she'd gladly have stuck pins in that guy's effigy."

Eric Mooney didn't own waterfront property. His home was on the eastern side of the road, and he may or may not have had water rights. Kathy knew that some people did and some people didn't.

Eric lived just south of Anissa's home, which was located on the water. Her father's dock had fallen into disrepair years before, so he—and now she—kept the boat at Tori's marina.

The women stopped in front of the decrepit building, where a tendril of smoke wafted from the structure's lone chimney. The clapboards hadn't seen a lick of paint in decades. Some of the asphalt shingles were curled and looked like a good stiff wind might rip them from the roof. Several windows had been boarded over, and the yard was littered with all kinds of junk, from rusty old vehicles to plastic lawn furniture and everything in between.

"Well, should we go up and knock?" Tori asked.

"I guess so," Kathy said with uncertainty.

The women walked through the wet grass that hadn't been mown in quite some time. Hopefully, tick season had passed, but Kathy was glad she'd worn socks and long pants.

Upon arriving at the door, Kathy turned to her friend. "Well, knock."

"You knock. You're the one who wants to offer him a job."

"Yeah, but you're the one who knows him."

Tori frowned but raised her arm, clenched her fist, and hammered on the door jamb and its peeling paint.

They waited in silence for at least half a minute before Kathy whispered, "Knock again."

Tori did so. Not long afterward, the door was wrenched open, and Eric Mooney stood before them bundled in a hoodie with the drawstring cinched under his neck, looking half frozen.

"Hey, Tori, what brings you here?"

"Hey, Eric, this is my friend and roommate, Kathy Grant. She owns Swans Nest Inn."

"Yeah, I've seen you gardening sometimes when I've been fishing on the bay bridge."

Kathy suddenly felt self-conscious. She had never considered that the fishermen might be watching her from afar.

"What brings you ladies here?"

Kathy's gaze drifted to what was left of a cord of wood. Was the ramshackle cottage heated only by a wood stove too small for the leaky structure? Would a man without an income freeze to death come winter?

"I see you're heating your house. We decided we're not turning on the heat until the first," Tori said.

Eric laughed. "When you're cold, you're cold. I've had a fire most mornings for the past couple of weeks." Just the mornings? "Once winter hits, I block off all the rooms and live in the kitchen. This'll be my fourth year. I've got it down pat," he said with a shrug.

"Maybe you can fix things up if you had a job," Kathy said.

"Yeah, and who's going to hire me?"

"Well, The Bay Bar is looking for someone to bus tables. It's only minimum wage, but it's a start," Tori said.

"Yeah, Noreen—one of the owners—told me that a few of their servers started as busboys or girls and ended up as servers. Tips can be really good during the summer months. And, apparently, servers are supposed to give you fifteen percent of their tips, too."

"Really?" Tori asked, sounding surprised.

Kathy shrugged. "Apparently."

"How's business in the winter?" Eric asked with a hint of an edge.

"I've only worked there two nights, so I don't have that kind of insight," Kathy admitted.

"I dunno," Eric said with a shrug.

"Well, if you're interested, you can show up around four this afternoon. Wear a white T-shirt and black pants if you've got them," Kathy said neutrally. She'd done her duty. It was now up to Eric to either accept or reject the offer.

"We'd better get going," Tori said. "It's almost time for me to call my Gramps."

"Say hi to him for me," Eric said

"Sure thing," Tori said.

The women turned and headed back down the road. When they reached the bend in the road, Kathy looked over her shoulder to see that Eric was still standing where they'd left him, watching them.

~

AS THE SEASONS CHANGED, Sundays around the Cannon Compound changed, too. Gone were early-bird bait customers, gasoline sales, and guys with fishing poles and tackle boxes in hand renting Tori's small fleet of boats.

One constant for all seasons was that Tori's grandfather called to see how things were going at the old family homestead. Usually, Tori enjoyed those calls, but she knew this conversation wasn't likely to be entirely pleasant. So, when the landline rang, Tori practically jumped. She picked up the receiver, knowing she was going to get a tongue-lashing.

"Hey, Gramps. What's up?" she asked with forced cheer.

"I was hoping you were going to tell me," Herb Cannon said forcefully.

"About what?" Tori asked innocently.

"Tor-ee," Herb said, drawing her name out.

"Oh, you mean the little bit of trouble we had here on Thursday?" she said and kind of laughed.

"*Little?*" Herb asked.

"Well, it wasn't *my* trouble."

"Anissa's trouble *is* your trouble because it happened on *our* property."

Whose property? Herb had deeded it to Tori for the grand sum of one dollar the previous fall.

Thanks to a network of informants, Herb's live-in lady friend, Irene, knew everything that happened in Ward County. Tori suspected Irene was in contact with other locals through every communication route and social media entity on the planet. Irene had no doubt heard about Tori and Anissa finding the dead man no sooner than it had been reported on the police scanner. Herb had probably been fuming for days, waiting for an update from Tori, who doubted she knew any more than Irene.

"We found the boat floating out on the bay with a dead guy in it. That doesn't mean he was dumped there while the boat was in our slip. Anissa hadn't used it in a couple of weeks."

"And *you* don't keep track of that?"

"Well, sort of. I mean, Ed Taylor took his boat to Toronto for a week and didn't tell me."

"And you didn't think to check?"

"I left a message on his answering machine, but it was a landline, and he didn't return it until after he got home. The boat was back a week later, and all was fine."

"Not for the guy with fried hands," Herb pointed out.

Tori winced at the memory of charred fingers.

"Truthfully, Gramps, I've been trying *not* to think about that poor man."

"You saw him, huh?"

"Oh, yeah. And have had nightmares about it ever since."

"Uh-huh," Herb said. Why couldn't he have shown just a little empathy for her experience? "So, what are you doing about the situation?"

"What do you mean?"

"I know you, girl. You've probably been poking your nose around trying to figure out what happened to the dead guy."

"No, I haven't," Tori said and didn't even have to fib.

"That's not what Irene tells me."

Did the woman have surveillance cameras trained on the house, the bait shop, and the Lotus Lodge—or were all three wired for sound?

"Well, she's mistaken. My interest is only related to the problem as it relates to Anissa."

"They ain't gonna charge her, are they?"

"Of course not! She didn't have anything to do with what happened to that poor man."

"I'm sure she didn't," Herb said, and the words sounded sincere. He, too, was fond of Anissa.

"But you know how things are in Ward County," Tori said. Yeah, where racism was alive and well. Well, not on the Cannon Compound!

"Yeah," Herb said, resigned. "I do. Anything else happening around there?"

Tori told him about Kathy's winter job—and the fact that she'd signed up to substitute teach once again.

"Do you need money?" Herb asked in a tone that sounded like the answer had better be *No*!

"Nope. I just want to finish the boathouse. Anissa's almost completed the work. She won't let me in because she wants to do a grand reveal like they do on TV home improvement shows."

"Well, why don't you film it? Get Kathy to hold the phone to record it so I can see your reaction as it happens."

"Can do," Tori said, sounding—and feeling—a little more cheerful.

"Is there a chance you could rent it over the winter?" Herb asked.

"Not this year. I mean, I'd have to turn on the water and heat it for the season without much hope of even a fifty percent occupancy. Besides, I still need to furnish it. I want to take my time to get it right. Maybe go to a few auctions and find a few antiques and some neat decorations."

"Sounds like you've got everything figured out," Herb said.

"Yeah, I'm a chip off the old Cannon block." Tori bet that down in Florida, her Gramps was smiling. Too bad she wasn't. "What's going on with you and Irene?" she asked.

"Not much. Life is pretty slow down here with no fear of a frost."

Tori said nothing.

"Irene's gonna be a grandmaw again."

"When?" Tori asked, trying to muster some enthusiasm.

"I don't pay all that much attention," Herb admitted. "But we're coming up on Tuesday because there's a baby shower next Sunday and she wants to help decorate the nursery."

Tori's heart sank. *Both of them?* "Well, I'm happy for her," Tori said.

"Yeah, she's as happy as a pig in poop."

It was a phrase Tori never truly understood.

"*We* may have to come back up when the baby arrives, too—first week in December," Herb amended. Usually, Irene traveled back to Ward County alone.

"Great." Tori wasn't sure where the couple would stay. Until the boathouse was available for guests—or the long-awaited reopening of The Lotus Lodge—they'd probably have to stay in an air B&B or with one of Irene's relatives, as there were no motels in the area.

"What time does your flight get in?" Tori asked. If she had to fetch the couple from the airport, it would eat up hours, and she couldn't work at the school.

"Around eleven. We're renting a car, so you don't have to come get us," Herb said.

"Well, you know I'd be happy to do so," Tori said.

"Gets a might crowded for three in that old truck," Herb muttered.

Good point. And now Tori had an excuse *not* to trade it in for anything else for the foreseeable future.

"I wish you'd keep me in the loop more often," Herb said sounding, disappointed.

"Sorry, Gramps. But we can catch up on Tuesday," Tori said. Did her grandfather hear the note of defeat in her voice?

"We need to carve out some time for you, me, and Anissa to

talk about the Lotus Lodge. Goodness knows it should have happened long before now," Herb said.

Except Tori knew the boathouse project would be finished faster than the seven-unit motel. And as it would bring in more rental income, it was a prudent decision. Still, Herb was putting up the money for that project. It would have been easier on Tori's pocketbook if refurbishing the motel had come first. Either way, neither project was likely to bring in any income until the following spring—if not summer.

"Gettin' to be lunchtime," Herb said. "I'd better let you go. But if anything else comes up, I expect to hear from you PDQ." It wasn't a statement or request. It was a direct order.

"Yes, Gramps," Tori dutifully said.

"Good."

"I love you, Gramps."

"And I love you, too," Herb said, his tone softening.

"See you on Tuesday," Tori promised.

"Good-bye," Herb said.

"Bye, Gramps," Tori said and ended the call. She sat there for a few long moments, feeling drained. How sad that her grandfather had fallen into a lot of money with a lottery win after a lifetime of struggling to make ends meet. That he had gifted her the property and was willing to bankroll the Lotus Lodge's revival was a godsend. But truthfully, Tori would much rather take that renovation on by financing it herself. She was between a rock and the proverbial hard place. She didn't have the cash to move forward with the project, and if her grandfather coughed up the cash, she would feel even more indebted to him. Still, it would take years for her to afford that renovation. And as her grandfather was at odds with most of the family, who thought they deserved a cut, she was grateful he still found time for her.

Tori stared at the phone, remembering that Eric Mooney had asked to be remembered to her grandfather. Well, if he stopped by the compound during the next week, he could do it himself.

Tori got up and looked out the window, studying the yard. If her grandfather was going to show up in just two days, she had better make the place inspection ready because Herb had a sharp eye and wasn't opposed to commenting (a kinder word than criticizing) what he saw as shortfalls.

So, Tori donned her jacket, grabbed a pair of gardening gloves, and headed outside to give the yard what might be the final weed whacking of the season.

She wasn't about to give her grandfather one extra thing to comment on.

∽

KATHY SHOWED up at The Bay Bar five minutes before four o'clock. A glance around the dining room told her there was no sign of Eric Mooney. Well, she hadn't really expected him to show up.

She found Noreen sitting at the far end of the bar, nursing a glass of ginger ale.

"Hey, girl," Kathy said, "what's up?"

"Hey, Kath. Sit down. Want something to drink?"

"No, thanks," Kathy said, slipping onto the stool beside Noreen.

"I spoke to Barb this afternoon," Noreen began.

"And?"

"We're good to go for Saturday."

"Great," Kathy said with forced enthusiasm.

"What have you got in mind for decorations?" Noreen asked.

Kathy frowned. "I don't provide them. It's the family or the bridesmaids who do that."

Noreen looked disappointed. "I just assumed you'd have everything like that available."

Kathy shook her head. "Nope." She was providing a space at a discounted rate. What did Noreen expect? When the bar hosted parties, Kathy was sure Noreen didn't supply decorations, either. "How many people are you expecting at the shower?"

"At least ten—possibly fifteen."

Kathy nodded. The front parlor could accommodate at least 15 people. It was doable.

"What kind of drinks will you be serving?" Kathy asked warily.

"Just coffee, tea, and water."

Kathy nodded. She'd supply tap water—she already knew she wouldn't make a penny of profit on this party, but she valued Noreen's friendship enough not to bring it up and supposed Noreen would bring her own coffee station to Swans Nest.

"Great."

Noreen nodded but then looked away, embarrassed. "Um, Ashley, one of former servers and a favorite with customers, had a baby last year but now she wants to come back to work at the bar on weekends."

That didn't sound good. "And?" Kathy asked.

"I was wondering if you'd prefer to work during the week."

Sure, there'd be less customers and the tips were sure to be low, if not non-existent. "Well," Kathy began.

"Ashely was one of our best servers. She could upsell steaks to toothless babies."

And Kathy would never feel comfortable doing anything of the sort.

"And this would leave you free to host weekend events like Barb's wedding shower at Swans Nest on the weekends."

Sure it would. Except ... such bookings were rare during the long, lean winter months.

Kathy bit her lip. She liked Noreen and Paul, but she could see that having an experienced server during their busiest evenings during their own lean times was sure to be a lot more attractive than someone like Kathy, who was too soft-hearted to try to take advantage of people who may or may not be able to afford to spend more than they could afford on a night out.

Kathy swallowed her disappointment. "So, when do you want me to work from now on?"

"I was thinking Tuesday through Thursday during the evening with an extra shift for the Friday lunch trade."

Siberia. But then, Kathy didn't have much to do during those hours except take care of her own and Tori's laundry and dust the furniture at Swans Nest. "Sure," she said brightly, feeling like she'd had the rug pulled out from under her and that Noreen was really pushing the boundaries of friendship.

Kathy decided right then that she would give the plan a couple of weeks, and if it didn't pan out, she would look for something else during the week. Maybe she could clean homes or sew curtains—anything to keep herself afloat during the long, cold winter.

"Great," Noreen said, smiling. "Now, while we're slow, why don't you do your side work." Wrapping a knife and fork inside a paper napkin wasn't a job Kathy enjoyed.

"Sure," she said again.

The door opened, and a blast of cold air *whooshed* around the bar. Eric Mooney entered the place. As Kathy had suggested the day before, he'd shown up in a clean white shirt and dark slacks. "Hey, Kathy," he called.

Kathy motioned him to join her and Noreen, where she introduced them.

Noreen explained what the job entailed and what it paid. Eric nodded throughout the recitation.

"Why don't I show you the ropes, and if you like the job, we'll go through the paperwork tomorrow," Noreen suggested.

Kathy frowned. Shouldn't she hire the guy before making him work a shift? She was about to say something but then bit her tongue. She believed Noreen would make good paying Eric for his work, but Kathy wasn't sure she trusted the woman. For some reason, Noreen seemed intent on cutting corners for a family member and making a deal that was detrimental to Kathy's bottom line. And then there was the whole debacle the previous spring when Noreen had asked Kathy to accommodate her overflow guests, who'd trashed Kathy's best suite. Noreen had made good paying for the damage, but it still bugged Kathy like a sore tooth.

Business was business, Kathy decided. But she didn't have to like the way it often turned out.

While Noreen showed Eric the job duties, Kathy retreated to the table at the side of the bar and started assembling the cutlery. They'd need at least fifty sets of the things.

But as she worked, Kathy fought tears. What had she expected? That this job could actually save her and Swans Nest?

At that moment, she had nothing but doubts.

CHAPTER 7

Tori was awake Monday morning at 5 am, eager to see if she'd be gainfully employed that day. In the past, the phone would ring, but recently, the school district had been emailing or texting to see if substitute teachers were available. She'd been called in a couple of times several weeks before and had gone on hiatus after an unpleasant encounter with one of the school's jocks. Now, she felt she had no choice but to return to teaching if she was going to survive the winter.

Tori fired up her computer, opened her email, retrieving the message that landed in her inbox ten minutes before, her heart sinking. Once again, she'd been assigned Mrs. Ellison's twelfth-grade English class. Mrs. Ellison seemed to be having a lot of health problems of late, which wasn't surprising as the woman was nearly eight months pregnant. Tori felt sure too many of those days off could be classified as mental health days because of one obnoxious student.

Bradley Hughes, a football jock, apparently suffered from an overload of testosterone and an ego the size of Alaska. The students and teachers deemed him a bully. He'd apparently been coddled since birth. He might be a gridiron star, but he teetered on the edge of being cut from the team for his educational inadequacies.

Though the school year had barely started, Tori had taken over the class on two previous occasions, and the boy—in age only, for he stood at least ten inches taller than Tori—had acted up both times.

Dressed all in black, Tori stood before the class, spine straight, her dark-framed glasses perched on her nose, determined to look formidable. She wasn't about to take any crap from Bradley. She waited for Mrs. Ellison's ten o'clock class to finish filing in and taking their seats, eyeing the clock before she took roll. Bradley was thankfully missing. Skipping school or just skipping class? She didn't care. With the man/boy gone, her anxiety almost dropped into her comfort zone.

"Hey, class," she began. "Mrs. Ellison's lesson plan calls for us to discuss chapter five of your current read, *Great Expectations*. Does anybody have an opinion on why Mrs. Joe allowed Joe to take Pip to look for the convicts?"

Several female students raised their hands while the guys averted their gazes—meaning they hadn't read the assignment. So, what else was new?

Tori consulted the seating chart. "Sophie?"

The strawberry blonde practically exploded with enthusiasm. Nothing brought Tori pleasure like the sight of a teen who'd embraced the assignment and obviously enjoyed relating the experience. Mrs. Ellison must be pretty proud of her girls.

Sophie was halfway through her answer when the classroom door opened, and Bradley Hughes walked in with a swagger and a sneer on his face, and five minutes late. Ward County High's football team lost a game the previous Saturday. Tori heard Bradley rushed for 52 yards but apparently fumbled the ball on the last play, and the team lost by three points. He was the school's hero and the senior class's top tormentor. Tori stared at the jock as he took his assigned seat but said nothing, her attention on the rest of Sophie's recitation.

"Excellent. Thank you, Sophie."

"Stupid," Bradley muttered.

Tori frowned. "What was that, Mr. Hughes?"

Bradley straightened in his seat. "The book. The whole premise is stupid."

"And why is that?" Tori asked, keeping her voice level.

Bradley glowered at her. "This *class* is stupid. If it wasn't mandatory, I'd be out of here."

"Well, if you really feel that way, feel free to leave," Tori said simply.

Bradley looked around the room at his classmates. Some of the guys nodded as though to egg him on. "Maybe I will."

"Just so you know, if you leave, I'll have to mark you absent. That information will be sent to the front office. They will decide how to deal with your choice."

"Are you threatening me?" Bradley asked, his voice taking on an edge.

"No, just telling you the facts," Tori said calmly. She saw a couple of the girls slip their hands into their purses and retrieve their phones—something that was forbidden during class. Still, if Bradley was about to make a scene, then Tori wasn't about to chastise them for breaking the rules by taking video of what might escalate to a confrontation.

Confrontation? That was the last thing Tori wanted. But she didn't want to deal with Bradley, either. If he left the room, she'd have a better chance of controlling the class, and actual learning might just take place.

"Now, class, as Sophie mentioned," Tori began.

"Who gives a shit what Sophie said," Bradley began.

"Profanity is not acceptable in my class," Tori said bluntly.

"This isn't *your* class. You're just a *sub*," Bradley sneered.

"I am filling in for Mrs. Ellison until she can return," Tori said firmly.

"If she shits that watermelon today, that could be months away," Bradley scoffed, with his buddies tittering in the background.

"You've now used profanity twice in this class. I told you that it is not acceptable. Would you please leave and report to the principal's office?"

"No!" Bradley asserted. "I won't."

More titters of laughter from a couple of the guys echoed through the room.

Tori gulped a deep breath, trying to stay calm. She walked over to the closed door and opened it. "Please leave before I'm forced to call security."

Bradley looked around at his buddies as though to get their permission, then nodded. "Okay, I'll leave," he said and strode forward, nodding his big blond head, but at least he was complying with Tori's request.

She stood by the door, keeping her expression passive. No way did she want to further challenge this bully. But as Bradley passed her, his arm flew up, fist clenched, and smacked her right on the nose before escaping.

The blow sent Tori staggering—hard—into the door. A couple of the girls cried out as Tori's legs buckled, and she slid to the cold tile floor, a fountain of blood gushing onto her face and dripping onto her turtleneck. Thank goodness it was black, she thought. She could probably save it from terminal stains.

"Ms. Cannon, Ms. Cannon! Should we call nine one one?" one of the girls called shrilly.

Tori pressed the folds of her turtleneck against her face, too stunned to think how she should answer.

Another girl crouched beside Tori, pressing an open packet of tissues into her free hand. Tori pulled the whole wad out of the plastic and plastered it against her face. It didn't seem to staunch the flow of blood.

Suddenly, Jim Bailey, one of the school's other English teachers, arrived, grabbed Tori by the biceps, and pulled her to her feet. "Are you okay, Tori?"

"I don't know," Tori said thickly, feeling decidedly spacy.

"Come on, let's get you down to the nurse's office," Jim said kindly before turning on the class. "The rest of you—take your seats, and don't you dare leave this room."

"I caught the whole thing on my phone," a female voice called out.

"So did I," another echoed.

"Save it for the police," Jim ordered.

Tori caught sight of the crowd of students. The threat that Bradley could be charged with assault had widened their eyes with shock.

Still holding the wad of tissues to her nose, Tori let Jim guide her out of the room to the stairwell, holding onto her as they descended the steps. Her Gramps was due to arrive the next day. How was she going to explain this to him? For that matter, how was she going to explain it to the principal that Bradley had so easily usurped her authority? If she couldn't keep the students in check, would they even let her back in the classroom? She needed this job to stay afloat over the winter.

As Tori and Jim entered the nurse's office, Tori wondered with dread if she'd soon be donning a Bay Bar t-shirt alongside Kathy—just to make ends meet.

~

"IT'S NOT BROKEN," Tori told her roommate while Kathy took in her swollen face and the dark circles under her eyes that were already beginning to appear. "They sent me to St. Jerome's ... just to make sure."

"'Sit down—sit down,' Kathy encouraged, helping Tori settle into one of the kitchen's maple chairs. "Can I get you anything? An icebag? A steak?"

Tori sighed. "No." Then she thought better of it. "Yes. A drink. A stiff one, please."

Kathy winced. "Sorry. All we've got is that nearly empty bottle of Asti Spumante."

"Not good enough," Tori said with a careful shake of her head.

Kathy frowned. "I could treat you to a drink at The Bay Bar."

"No, you couldn't. You need every penny you made in tips so far to keep afloat."

"This occasion calls for something to mitigate it," Kathy said.

Tori's head dipped. Yeah, it did. They wouldn't have to worry about that kind of slight indulgence if they weren't so overextended. "What worries me is that Gramps is due to arrive tomorrow. I can just imagine how he's going to react to this."

"Now, don't go borrowing trouble. Just tell him you ran into a door."

"Like he's going to believe that," Tori grumbled.

"A rake?"

Tori shook her head.

"At least you don't have to pick him and Irene up at the Rochester airport."

"True, but I don't think the district is going to let me go back to substitute teaching until the bruising subsides. Today, it's nothing. By tomorrow, I'm going to look like a raccoon—or at least half my face will."

"They ought to give you combat pay. You ought to threaten to at least sue that jock's parents for the assault."

"I'm pretty sure I'd have a case. A couple of the students took videos. I had the nurse at the hospital take pictures. You can also take pictures as the bruising develops tomorrow and over the next few days."

"You bet I will. That kid needs to be taught a lesson—an

expensive one. Not only monetarily, but that actions have consequences."

"You mean like being kicked off the football team?"

"Exactly." Kathy cocked her head, taking in Tori's swollen face once more. "I can afford to pay for one round at the bar. Let's go now, and then we'll come back, and I'll whip up something for us—if nothing else, tuna sandwiches."

The cupboards were pretty bare. Tori planned to hit the grocery store in Warton the next day before her grandfather arrived. She wanted to make sure he saw a fully stocked fridge lest he think she couldn't fend for herself.

"It's pretty early. Is the bar even open?"

"Of course they are." Kathy rose from her chair. "Come on." She offered a hand to help Tori up but was refused. Tori had a bruised face, but she wasn't an invalid.

That said, when Noreen saw Tori's swollen face, she—who never had a child—immediately morphed into a mother hen.

"Goodness! What happened to you?" she cried as Tori settled onto one of the barstools.

"My nose met a clenched fist."

"One of the high schoolers made a painful impression on Tor," Kathy explained, taking the stool beside Tori.

"Let me get you some ice," Noreen said, grabbed a towel, and dug a shovel full of ice from the well behind the bar, wrapping it up and handing it to Tori. "That should help. Now, what can I get you girls?"

"I'll take a margarita," Tori said.

"Make that two," Kathy agreed.

"Coming right up," Noreen said, hauling out a couple of margarita glasses, dipping them in salt, and making the drinks before delivering them on white cocktail napkins.

"Now, tell Mama Noreen what happened."

Tori did just that, adding that her grandfather would arrive the next day.

"We haven't seen Herb in a coon's age. You've gotta bring him over. If only for one of our fish fries. If he can't make it on Friday, I'll make sure to have it available on whatever day he can make it."

"I know he'd like that. He mentioned he can't get anything like it in Florida."

Noreen winked. "I got him covered."

A couple of guys dressed in black leathers entered the bar. "Back to work," Noreen said, took the guys order of a couple of beers and then delivered them to where they'd taken up cues to play a game of 8 Ball. After that, she left them to go back behind the grill to flip burgers and make fries.

Tori sipped her margarita, noticing Kathy staring at the now-closed door to the kitchen. "Anything wrong?"

Kathy frowned. "Not wrong, just—" she paused, "—kind of weird."

"In what way?"

"Noreen's been kind of cool toward me since I started working here; but you come in, and she fawns all over you."

Tori shrugged. "Maybe she feels she needs to keep you at arm's length because you're now her employee instead of a friend."

"Maybe," Kathy said, but didn't sound convinced.

Tori probed the swelling under her right eye and winced. "How long does it take bruises to heal?"

Kathy let out a breath. "A couple of weeks."

Tori's gaze dipped. "So, I could be out of work for half a month?"

"Maybe," Kathy said quietly. "You could devote yourself to making pendants for your Etsy shop. Christmas is right around the corner," she quipped cheerfully.

Yeah, and there were probably a hundred other crafters on the shopping website making broken china pendants, earrings, and bracelets.

"Maybe you could do some tutoring? You could put up a sign at Tom's Grocery with tabs with your phone number."

"Maybe," Tori said, not feeling the love for that suggestion.

"There you are," came a voice from the doorway. Anissa stepped forward and plopped down on a barstool next to Kathy. She did a double-take when she saw Tori's face. "What on earth happened to you, girlfriend?"

Kathy's expression soured. "One of her students mistook her for a punching bag."

"I'll say," Anissa said.

"Anything new with you?" Tori asked.

Anissa frowned. "Just more questions from Detective Osborn. He showed up at my job site. How did that guy know where to find me? Do you think he placed a tracker on my truck or something?"

"Maybe he's psychic," Kathy said. "What did he want?"

"Probably to pin that fried guy's death on me."

Noreen peeked through the round window in the kitchen's swinging door, saw Anissa, and reentered the restaurant. "What can I get you, Anissa?"

"Nothing, thanks. I just came over to find these little gals and maybe hang out for a few hours."

"You're more than welcome to join us for supper," Kathy said. "We're having tuna sandwiches and chips, although they may be a bit stale."

"You guys always make me feel welcome," Anissa said.

Tori drained her glass. "I'm ready to go home. Maybe I'll beat my head against the wall until it makes me feel better."

"You won't do any such thing," Kathy admonished. She polished off the rest of her drink and pulled out her wallet.

Noreen stepped forward, waving her hand. "Nope. You're not paying for those drinks. Consider them for medicinal purposes."

"Aw, you don't have to do that," Kathy said sincerely.

Noreen brandished an evil smile. "Don't worry, you'll work it off on your next shift."

Yeah, she probably would.

"Thanks, Noreen. You're a good friend," Tori said.

"I aim to please," she said cheerfully.

The women left the bar and crossed the street to retreat to Tori's bungalow, passing Anissa's truck, which was parked just outside the house—not her usual spot to leave it. Tori unlocked the door, switched on the kitchen light, and entered. Kathy and Anissa followed. After hanging their jackets on a peg near the door, Tori and Anissa took seats at the table.

"I wish we had a nice cold bottle of wine," Tori lamented. "That margarita wasn't nearly enough to drown my sorrows."

"How come?" Anissa asked as Kathy gathered plates from the cupboard.

Tori began her tale of woe. She hadn't gotten far into her recitation when Kathy interrupted.

"Hey, did you go grocery shopping, Tor?"

Tori frowned. "No. Not only didn't I have time, but there isn't enough in my checking account to cover using my debit card. Why?"

"Because the cupboard is stocked. And—" Kathy flung open the fridge, which was also packed full with a gallon of milk, bags of fresh produce, and packages of meat, as well as a couple of bottles each of red and white wine. "How the heck...?" Kathy muttered.

"Elves?" Anissa suggested. Tori and Kathy turned confused gazes on their friend. "You know, like *The Elves And The Shoemaker*. There was a need, and it was fulfilled," Anissa explained.

Tori blinked. "Oh, Anissa. You didn't have to do this."

"Yes, I did," she said sincerely. "You gals have fed me on countless occasions. But more importantly, you've been the best friends I could have asked for." She turned her gaze on Tori. "You told people I was a contractor. Without that endorsement, I wouldn't have found enough gainful employment to stay independent. I would have had to sell my Daddy's house here on the bay and go back to living in a crappy apartment with a roommate."

"Not all roommates are bad," Kathy chirped.

"You guys buck the odds," Anissa said sourly. She hadn't been as lucky with former housemates.

"You didn't have to do that," Tori reiterated, her voice tightening with emotion.

"Well, it's done. And I'm not taking a damn thing back. And if y'all still want tuna sandwiches for supper, I wouldn't mind joining you." She eyed the top of the fridge where a big bag of barbeque potato ships sat. "Just to keep you company, you understand."

"Yeah," Kathy said. "We'd love your company."

Anissa nodded. "Is there anything I can do to help? Chop celery or onions?"

Kathy shook her head. "I've got everything under control," she said, taking a couple of cans of tuna out of the pantry.

Tori swallowed down the lump in her throat, catching Anissa's gaze. *Thank you*, she mouthed.

Anissa reached out a hand and gave Tori's a squeeze. "No, thank *you*."

Tori nodded.

Anissa smiled and looked beyond her friend and in Kathy's direction. "If you peek inside the freezer, you might just find a bottle of white wine just chillin' faster than the others. That is if you're thirsty."

"I'm thirsty," Kathy agreed, turning to grab three wine glasses from the cupboard.

"Me, too," Tori agreed.

And the day went from being crap as the light of friendship cracked the smothering cloak of doom that had engulfed her most of the day.

CHAPTER 8

No message came from the school district the following day asking Tori to substitute teach, and since she hadn't set the alarm on her phone, she ended up sleeping in late—that is, if you could call seven o'clock late.

Tori got up and decided to open the bait shop, not that she expected many (any?) customers. But she had a few regulars who bought bait and snacks after Labor Day weekend.

Kathy hadn't emerged from her bedroom, so after fortifying herself with a big mug of hot tea and one of Kathy's savory sundried tomato muffins slathered with butter, Tori quietly left the bungalow and headed for the bait shop.

Inspecting her reflection on the shop's plate glass door, Tori decided there was no way she could return to school with her swollen and blackened eye. Maybe by the following Monday, she could apply a thick coat of foundation and disguise what was left of the bruise. She'd have to wait and see. But staying home also meant four days without pay. And how would she explain to her grandfather how she'd received the injury?

Tori was glad her grandfather and Irene didn't need to be picked up from the Rochester airport. She was also grateful the bungalow was too small to accommodate guests and that Irene had booked an AirBnB for their stay. Tori wondered if she could put Herb off from visiting the compound for a few days until the worst of the swelling went down. And maybe hell would freeze over, too.

Tori looked out the bait shop's window to the refurbished boat house and its luxury accommodations. Too bad the timing of its completion was off. She'd have to wait at least six months before she could rent it out and start to see a return on her hefty investment.

Tori looked out onto the water and gray sky beyond. Was she likely to see *any* customers on this cold and blustery day? Probably not. But she could work on her broken-china jewelry, add photos of the pieces to her Etsy store, and cross her fingers they'd sell during the holiday season.

She'd been concentrating on attaching the silver edging around one of her heart designs when the shop's door opened. It was Eric Mooney, holding the same plastic bucket she surmised was filled with fish.

"Got a good catch?" Tori asked.

"Only bluegills, but I've got me a tasty breakfast." It had been less than an hour since Tori had had her nine millionth muffin. Kathy was constantly testing new recipes, and Tori was her guinea pig. She accepted the role, but eating the same thing every morning became tiresome.

Taking in her bruised face, Eric seemed to do a doubletake. "What happened to you? Did you walk into a door?"

"Something like that," Tori said. Until then, she hadn't considered how her appearance might put off customers. Would they think she was careless or a victim of domestic violence? It had been violence, all right, and she was still considering taking legal action against the man-sized kid.

"I hear you're doing well at The Bay Bar," she remarked.

"Yeah, thanks to you and Kathy, things are really looking up for me," Eric said, grinning.

Tori smiled. "I'm so glad to hear that."

Eric nodded. "Now that I'm working, I want to upgrade the old homestead. I've seen the changes you've made to the compound." He laughed. "You're my inspiration."

A gush of pride coursed through Tori. "Thanks. I've worked hard to bring the business back into the black."

"I'm also inspired by what your friend—the black chick—has done to her house to bring it back to life. That's what I want to do with my place."

"I'm sure you'll accomplish all that," Tori said with what she hoped was sincerity. The old Mooney home really was a pit.

"I've got a long list of repairs to make, but I figure I'll have to work a few months to save up to make them. Any suggestions on what I should do first?"

Boy, was he jumping the gun. He'd only worked two shifts at The Bay Bar, and he was already making grand plans for his minimum-wage spoils. Still, Tori answered honestly.

"If your place isn't watertight, it's gonna rot," she said honestly. "Get any roof leaks fixed before winter comes, even if it's just a patch job. Then, when you're more financially stable, you can attack bigger projects. But there's a lot you can do that won't cost a dime to give your place more curb appeal."

"And that is?"

"Clean up the yard." The grass hadn't been mown in ages, and all sorts of useless items were scattered amongst the weeds.

"I don't have a way to get rid of the stuff."

"I've got a pickup. You can toss the stuff in my truck bed, and we can take it to the dump."

Eric blinked. "You'd do that for me?"

"Why not? You're my neighbor, right?"

Sort of.

"I'd really appreciate that."

"I've got a weed whacker I can loan you to knock down the

worst of the grass. After that, maybe we can figure out how to get your lawn back under control." Anissa might be willing to loan him her lawnmower—which Herb had given her the year before. She'd ask before she volunteered Anissa's property.

"Thanks, Tori. You and Kathy are the best friends I have here on the bay."

Wow. And he'd only met Kathy two days before. Tori didn't reply to that statement.

Eric placed the bucket on the floor and shook his arm. "That thing's getting heavy. I ought to get home and cook these little guys—and if the rain holds off, I'll start on the yard."

"Sounds like a plan," Tori said brightly.

Eric nodded. "Thanks again." He picked up the bucket once more.

"See you soon," Tori said. Eric nodded, and she watched him leave the shop, heading across the gravel path toward Resort Road.

Eric was the same age as Tori, but she always thought of him as being far younger—probably because he had a baby face. He sure hadn't made much of his life. He seemed to be surfing through it, never diving into the metaphorical waters to find depth and meaning—and possibly treasure.

Such were the thoughts of a woman who sold worms, maggots, and minnows. But Tori had ambition. It wasn't a dirty word when applied to men, but women who shared that emotion were often called bitches and looked down upon.

Screw that.

Again, Tori looked out the window toward the boathouse. Her vision and her hard-earned cash had gone into the project. She would make sure the venture succeeded.

She had to.

~

Since she hadn't had a customer all day, Tori closed the bait shop early and returned to the bungalow. She also hadn't heard a word from her grandfather, despite the fact his plane had landed on time around noon. Maybe that was a good thing. If he called tomorrow, she could say she wouldn't be available and at least stall him for another day.

It was almost four o'clock when Tori heard the sound of an engine and looked out the bungalow's front door's glass to see an unfamiliar car pull into the lot. The door opened, and Herb Cannon got out of the vehicle. In years past, he'd been known for wearing plaid flannel shirts, grease-stained overalls, and work boots. He'd updated his wardrobe since moving south and was decked out in a green golf shirt, khaki slacks, and polished dress shoes. Tori watched as he turned to take in the bay, his head swiveling to examine a vista he'd seen thousands of times before.

Kathy wandered into the kitchen, dressed in her oversized Bay Bar T-shirt that now fit snugly around her waist because she'd tied a knot in the fabric that rested on her left hip. "What's up?"

Tori sighed. "Gramps just arrived."

"Oh, boy," Kathy muttered. "How are you going to handle this?"

Tori shrugged. "I'll just have to wing it."

That sounded pretty glib when what Tori actually felt was terror. Her grandmother had given her unconditional love but she had to earn it—over and over again—from her grandfather.

"You answer the door," Tori said.

"Why me?"

"Because I want to delay explaining why I look like a punching bag for as long as possible."

"That's going to be about ten seconds," Kathy pointed out.

"That's ten seconds longer to give me time to think of how I'm going to explain what happened to me. And mark my words, Gramps is going to somehow pin the blame on me."

Kathy nodded knowingly and moved to stand before the door, while Tori stepped back and turned the unblemished side of her face toward the aperture.

Kathy straightened, turned the handle, and threw open the door. "Mr. Cannon, it's so good to see you," she said brightly. "Come on in."

Herb crossed the threshold, and Kathy lunged forward to hug the old man, which he reciprocated, although not nearly as effusively.

He looked over Kathy's shoulder at Tori. "And aren't you going to give your old gramps a hug, too, girl?" he said.

"I'm so glad to see you," Tori said, still turning her bruised eye away from him. Herb seemed to push Kathy away and made a beeline toward his granddaughter. But before he could take another step, the screen door to the kitchen opened again, and Anissa barged in.

"Mr. Cannan," she said, which caused Herb to turn in her direction.

"Hey, Anissa," and then Anissa stepped forward to give the old man a hug.

"How you doing? It's great to see you again."

"It's good to see you, too," Herb said, disentangling himself pretty quickly. "I just got here and I haven't yet had a chance to give my best girl a hug and kiss."

Anissa smiled. "Well, then, be my guest."

Tori's stomach tightened. She had mere seconds to come up with a story that might placate her all-too-judgmental grandfather.

Herb's mouth dropped open in shock as he took in Tori's bruised face. "What in God's name happened to you?" he thundered.

Tori looked away. "Oh ... one of my students—"

"A student gave you a shiner?" Herb asked, perturbed.

Tori shrugged. "He was disrupting the class. I asked him to go to the principal's office, and he declined. He was worried about being kicked off the football team."

"Tell me it was a skinny quarterback," Herb grated.

Tori's head dipped. "Uh, no. He's a linebacker. A six-foot two-inch behemoth."

"Oh, Tori," Herb wailed. Then he frowned, his gaze narrowing. "Are *you* in trouble over this?"

Sure. That had been Herb's first reaction when Tori lost her full-time teaching job the year before. He was sure she must have done something wrong rather than believe it was due to budget cuts.

"No," Tori said through gritted teeth. "The kid was suspended."

Herb didn't look convinced. "So, what are you going to do next?"

"Apply a thick coat of concealer and go back to teaching."

"Oh, no," Herb declared. "I don't want you going back to that school."

"But Gramps, that's how I make a living off-season."

"Not anymore," Herb stated.

Tori wasn't sure how to take that. Did he expect her to wait tables like Kathy during the off-season? Living off tips was even more precarious than substitute teaching. "In the future, I'll just specify working at the elementary or middle school."

"There are plenty of other jobs you could take," Herb proclaimed.

"Like what?"

"Well, Irene says Tom's Grocery store needs a new cashier."

Tori frowned.

"There's nothing wrong with that job. Or isn't it good enough for you?" Herb asked, annoyed.

"To keep this ship afloat, I need a more substantial job. Daisy and I need to eat, as well as pay the utilities."

"And your plan in the meantime?" Herb pressed.

Tori thought quickly. "I could contact my slip renters and offer them a discount if they pay up now for the summer season."

"And then what will you do next summer with no cash coming in?"

"By then I'll be renting the apartment over the boathouse. And hopefully the Lotus Lodge will be up and running, too."

"Hope don't pay the bills," Herb said tartly.

Tori held her tongue. She couldn't afford to alienate her grandfather. He'd been incredibly generous to her but also expected a lot in return.

"Would you like to see the apartment over the boathouse, Mr. Cannon?" Anissa asked as though to redirect Herb's attention. "I think you'll like what you see."

Herb's expression said no, but he grumbled a half-hearted "Okay."

"Follow me," Anissa said.

She led Herb, Tori, and Kathy across the expanse of lawn until they came to the boathouse, which had undergone quite a transformation since Herb had last seen it.

"That staircase ain't handicap accessible," he said grudgingly.

"No, it's not for everyone," Anissa agreed. "But for those with steady legs, it's a dream come true."

Herb looked unconvinced.

Anissa pulled a key from her pocket and unlocked the door at the top of the stairs. She, threw open the door and went inside with Herb right behind. Herb stopped so abruptly that Tori nearly crashed into him.

"Wow," Herb breathed, looking through the kitchen area to the floor-to-ceiling windows and French doors that overlooked the bay's west—burn—side. The colors were nowhere near at peak, but there was enough to hint at the spectacular vista to come.

Herb shook his head and looked around at the kitchen surrounding him. Granite counters flanked a high-end stainless-steel fridge, stove, and dishwasher. The cabinets were painted white, which made the room feel light and airy.

Anissa held out a hand, ushering the older gentleman into the living room. "We decided not to furnish the place until spring. No sense letting it sit in the damp until Tori can rent it next May."

Also, it made no sense to furnish the space until Tori could actually afford furniture.

Anissa opened one of the doors to the left. "This is the master suite," she said with a flourish. "The en suite boasts a walk-in shower with a rain head. We thought about putting in a claw-foot tub, but that's more the vibe over at Swans Nest," she said simply.

"I can't argue with that," Herb said, his voice considerably lower than it had been just minutes before.

"There's also a secondary bedroom and bathroom," Anissa said, gesturing toward the opposite side of the living room. "It faces north. Picture it—late nights taking in the Northern Lights over Lotus Point."

"That sure would look pretty," Herb agreed.

Anissa ushered Herb toward the sliding glass doors that overlooked a deck. "Imagine sitting out on the desk taking in the sunset from June through September."

"And hopefully beyond," Tori piped up.

Herb nodded. "You've done a beautiful job, Anissa."

"Tori was the guiding force behind this renovation."

Kathy had helped, too, but Tori wasn't about to confess that. Right now, she needed her grandfather to see that she had things under control—or at least as much as she could muster under the circumstances.

"It's too bad you couldn't have had this finished before the end of the season," Herb told Tori.

"Anissa did her best. And we had to wait for materials and subcontractors to do some of the work."

"I predict that next season, Tori has a full house," Kathy piped up.

"I'll second that," Anissa agreed.

Herb had never been a fan of transforming the boathouse into a high-end rental. He took in all the top-quality finishes. "Maybe."

Tori changed the direction of the conversation. "Come and see how far we've come with the Lotus Lodge."

"Humph," was Herb's reply.

They excited the boathouse, trundled down the stairs, and made their way across the gravel parking lot to the old motel. The exterior still needed a lot of work, but once they entered the first unit, Herb looked just a little contrite. "It looks pretty good."

"We've upgraded the insulation, the wiring, the heating and cooling systems. All that's left to do is paint, install carpet, furnish the seven units, and buy a new washer and dryer to take care of the guest linens and towels."

Herb's expression soured. "And how will Tori take care of all that *and* the bait shop?"

"You never questioned how Grandma did it?" Tori retorted.

Herb didn't acknowledge the statement. "Are all the units in this condition?"

"Yup," Anissa said. "And Tori has a lot of linens and retro decorations ready to go up. There's no point in doing that work now. It can wait until spring."

Herb nodded. "You girls have done a good job," he grudgingly admitted.

Tori had to bite her tongue to not remind her grandfather that they were women, *not* girls. She decided to change the subject. "Let's go back to the house and have coffee and some of Kathy's lemon pound cake."

"That's the best offer I've had all week," Herb said.

The four returned to the bungalow and settled at the kitchen table. Soon, Kathy had the coffee percolating and was slicing pieces of cake she'd baked earlier.

"So, who's going to give me all the dirt on the dead guy?" Herb asked.

"We don't know much at all," Tori said, picking up a fork to cut a piece of the cake. "Just his name."

"Chuck Stanton," Herb stated and nodded. "I knew him pretty well."

"You did?" Tori asked, surprised.

"Oh, sure. He did a lot of work around the bay. Your grandma had him in for coffee and cake lots of times. His crew took care of the lines after storms for over twenty years. He knew more about handling 'lectricity than just about anybody. That's why I was shocked to hear he'd been fried."

Tori winced at the descriptor. She'd had a nightmare or two about seeing the man's body and wondered if the memory of the sight would haunt her for years to come.

"What was Mr. Stanton like?" Anissa asked.

Herb shrugged. "A nice enough guy. He came out here and hunted ducks up on Willow Point every fall. I guess he woulda done it next month if he hadn't been fried."

Tori winced. "Do you have to keep saying that?"

"What? That he was fried?" Herb asked, puzzled.

She nodded.

"Okay, that he was burned to death. That's what electrocution is, right?"

"Not exactly," Kathy piped up. "According to Tori, only his hands were burned. The electrical current disrupted his cardiac rhythms. *That's* what killed him."

Herb frowned. "Oh, so now you're a doctor?"

Kathy met his gaze. "No. I looked it up online."

"Well, goody for you," Herb said factiously, grabbed his cup, and gulped down the rest of his coffee.

The three women looked at each other, silently communicating that crossing Herb was not in Tori's best interest.

"How's the house you're staying in?" Anissa asked innocently.

"Expensive," Herb grumbled. He seemed to forget that he was now a multimillionaire since winning the New York State Lottery the year before.

"And what does Irene think of the place?" Anissa asked.

"Aw, she loves it. All those gewgaws on the walls and every flat surface." Herb turned to gaze toward the back of the bungalow—a place he'd shared with Tori's grandmother for over forty years. His eyes seemed unnaturally bright, perhaps shiny with unshed tears.

"And how're her other grandbabies?" Tori asked.

Herb frowned. "Ugly as sin. But they'll probably get cuter as they get older." He didn't sound quite sure of that. "Anyway, Irene is already talking about coming back for Christmas."

"I'm closed for the holidays," Kathy said, "but I'd be glad to host you with the friends and family discount," Kathy offered.

Herb looked at her with ... disappointment? Did he expect her to host him for free? "We'll see. Irene might come up by herself."

"You don't want to be alone down in Florida on Christmas Day, do you?" Tori asked.

Herb shrugged. "It's just another day to me." But then his gaze again traveled to the back of the bungalow and its living room, where Tori's grandmother used to set up her Christmas tree. "Anyway," he said and cleared his throat. "My favorite thing about Christmas wasn't the presents—cuz goodness knows I only ever got a few all the years I was growing up, and then it was likely to be underwear or socks. The best part was the food. The cookies. The roast turkey—or chicken if it was a tough year—and all the fixings." He shook his head, looking wistful. "Yeah, yer grandmaw made the best holiday meals."

From what Tori gathered, Irene wasn't much interested in

cooking and back in Florida she and Herb ate most of their dinners at places that offered early-bird specials.

"Well, let me know," Kathy said offhandedly and rose from the table, taking her empty cup and plate over to the sink to rinse off before stacking them in the dishwasher. She didn't return to join the others but leaned against the counter, arms crossed over her chest, staring at the fridge.

Tori knew that Kathy would pull out all the stops should Herb and Irene stay at Swans Nest. Judging by Kathy's reaction, Herb balking at paying stung. It wasn't something Tori wanted to discuss with her BFF.

"So, what's on tap for you tonight?" Tori asked her grandfather.

"On tap? I'd like to visit Paul and Noreen across the road for a few beers, but Irene's got me booked at her daughter's house. She's going to be making spaghetti and meatballs—from a jar and the frozen food case at Tom's Grocery in Warton."

"I'm sure her daughter will appreciate a night off cooking," Anissa said blandly.

Kathy remained silent.

Herb pushed his crumb-filled plate away and stood. "Well, I'd best be getting back to Becky's house for dinner."

"Will you come by tomorrow?" Tori asked. "I thought we might go fishing."

"Irene's got all these plans leading up to the shower on Sunday."

"And when are you guys going back to Florida?" Anissa asked.

"Our flight is at two o'clock Monday afternoon."

Tori nodded. Herb's whole visit was geared more toward Irene's family than spending time with his granddaughter on the compound. Well, she couldn't host her grandfather and his lady friend—at least not yet. Tori had always considered her grandfather to be the boss of his family. That Irene seemed to call all the shots in his life disturbed her. And yet, it was at Irene's insistence that Herb had deeded the Cannon Compound to Tori.

Tori popped up, kissed her grandfather on the cheek, and wrapped her arm around the old man's. "I'll walk you to your car."

Herb nodded in Kathy's and Anissa's direction. "See you gals later."

"Sure thing," Anissa said.

Kathy said nothing.

Tori accompanied Herb to the rental car, a tiny economy model. He probably didn't want to waste money on a more expensive vehicle he could well afford to rent. Well, it was hard to break the thrifty habits of one who'd grown up in poverty.

Herb got in the car, started it, and rolled down the window.

"I love you, Gramps."

Herb smiled. "And I love you, too, Tori."

"Please come back. I miss you." Left unsaid was, "You're the only family who cares about me." Did Herb get that?

"Don't worry, I'll be back."

Once or twice before he headed back to Florida?

Tori could only cross her fingers and hope.

CHAPTER 9

Kathy went to work; Anissa stayed for a fried egg sandwich and a couple of chess games before she headed for home, and Tori dragged herself off to bed. Much as she loved her grandfather, his visit had plunged her further into the throes of depression. As if that wasn't enough, she dreamed about Chuck Stanton's corpse, only this time, he rose from the bottom of Anissa's aluminum boat, his charred hands reaching to grab her.

It took a long time before she fell asleep once again.

No message from the school district landed in her inbox or in the form of a text message. Had Mrs. Ellison come back to work, or had Tori been abandoned by the district? She didn't want to contemplate that scenario.

As usual, Kathy slept in, and Tori made a pot of tea and sliced another hunk of the lemon pound cake for her breakfast before heading to the bait shop.

The bay was warmer than the air, and fog obscured Tori's regular vista. As the sun came out, it would burn off the mist. That is *if* the sun came out. At that time of year, it was never a given.

That day, Tori decided to work on earrings to match some of her most recent pendants. They could be sold individually or as a set. Sadly, she hadn't had an order in over two weeks. Would today be her lucky day?

She doubted it.

Tori listened to the Rochester soft-rock station as she worked, only really paying attention when the weather report came on: cloudy with stretches of sunshine. Well, it was better than rain—and far better than snow and ice, which would arrive all too soon.

Tori had just finished attaching silver earring hangers to heart-shaped dingle-dangles when she glanced out the bait shop's window and saw a pontoon boat nudging one of the slips on her dock. She didn't own such a craft. Her rentals were all aluminum, between ten and fourteen feet long. She was pretty sure she knew who owned the boat and figured, as long as she hadn't had a customer all morning, she should return it to its rightful owner.

Putting a BE BACK SOON sign up on her door, she locked the bait shop, captured the pontoon's broken rope, tied another line to it, and then jumped into one of her rentals, fired up the motor, and chugged the length of the Bay bridge to her nearest competitor. She corralled the barge into one of the empty slips and tied it and her own boat up before trudging to the Bayside Live Bait & Marina.

"Hey, Don," she called once inside.

Don Newton, the building's proprietor, came out from the back room. It looked like he'd had just as many customers as Tori.

"Hey, Tor. I saw you pull up. Thanks for rescuing my escapee."

"Not a problem," she said.

Don winced, taking in her face. "That's quite the shiner you've got."

"Yeah," she said succinctly.

He didn't seem satisfied with that answer.

"Some guy beat you up?"

"Yeah, the captain of the Warton High School's football team."

"Bradley Hughes?" he asked, apparently surprised.

"You know him?" Tori asked.

"I know his dad. He's one of my regulars."

"Yeah, well, I'm still trying to decide if I should sue the family. If nothing else, I hope he gets some kind of punishment."

"That could ruin his life," Don said, rather taken aback.

"Yeah, and if he thinks he can abuse women at age eighteen and *never* have to answer for it, he's sadly mistaken," Tori said vehemently. Until that moment, she hadn't realized just how upset she was over the whole situation.

"Well, I'm sorry it happened."

Was he sorry the kid was in trouble, sorry she'd been injured, or sorry the end of Bradley's meaty, clenched fist had possibly ruined the kid's gridiron prospects?

She didn't ask.

Don changed the subject. "Heard you had some trouble over at the compound last week," he said casually.

"You mean the dead guy?"

Don nodded.

"Yeah. The poor man was electrocuted. I sure hope the cops don't try to pin it on Anissa Jackson."

"Why, because she's your friend?" The timbre of his voice set Tori's teeth on edge.

"I've known Anissa most of my life."

"No, you haven't. You knew her as a child. You've only reconnected in the past year or so."

"I know her character. She isn't the type to murder anyone."

"Well, someone killed that guy."

Yes, Chuck Stanton had died violently. But how would someone murder by electrocution?

The idea brought another thought to mind. Nobody had mentioned where Stanton's personal or company vehicle had been found. He didn't just walk from his home in Warton to the Cannon compound. It was a question she thought she'd ask Detective Osborn.

"Did you know Mr. Stanton well?"

"Chuck? Yeah. He was one of my semiregular customers. He used to show up five or six times a year and entered most of the derbies I run."

"Did he ever win?"

Don shrugged. "He came in second a couple of times." There was something about the man's tone that seemed off.

"And?" Tori asked.

"I couldn't prove it, because like I said, he never won any of those fishing contests, but it was said he used lead sinkers to cheat the system. But he was judicious enough never to overload the fish, so as far as I know, it was just rumors."

"And who'd spread those kinds of rumors?" Tori asked.

"Just a few of the regulars. I figured maybe Chuck had a few too many beers at The Bay Bar and might have let it slip. But like I said, I never caught him doing that."

Tori nodded. "His widow came to my place a few days ago. She was pretty upset."

"And why not? She'd just lost her husband."

"Yeah, but...." Tori didn't finish the sentence.

"But what?"

Tori shrugged. Something had seemed off when she'd spoken to Alice Stanton. She'd have to think about it.

"Well, anyway, your boat is back. Better give it a new rope."

"I'm hauling all my boats out next week anyway. How about you?"

"Yeah, maybe," Tori said. If she were to be locked out of substitute teaching and there wasn't another place to rent boats on the south end of the bay, she could afford to keep her boats in the water if Don beached his.

"Thanks for bringing back my pontoon," Don said again.

"You're welcome. Hope you have a great winter season."

"Same to you," Don said.

Tori nodded and exited the warm shop to be enveloped by the damp cold. She trundled down the dock, jumped into her boat, untied the rope, and backed out of the slip, turning the craft around to head across the expanse of water to her own dock, which took less than a minute.

So, Chuck Stanton might not have been the paragon of virtue his widow had proclaimed. Well, when someone lost the love of their life, they weren't inclined to acknowledge their flaws. Maybe Alice would see things differently in the years to come—and maybe she wouldn't. Tori wasn't about to judge the woman. The fact that more than one person suspected Chuck Stanton of cheating said something about his character. Still, was that enough for someone to kill the man?

Tori wasn't at all sure.

~

THE BAIT SHOP'S phone rang after hours, but Tori let it go to the old-fashioned answering machine her grandmother had installed years ago. At the *beep*, she heard Eric Mooney's voice. "Hey, Tori, I took your suggestion and cleaned up my yard. If you've got time in the next few days, I'd appreciate the use of your truck to take all this crap to the dump." He left his number and hung up.

Feeling dispirited, Tori decided to wait to answer the call just then, figuring she'd do it in the morning.

Kathy entered the kitchen. "Was that Eric's voice I heard?"

"Yeah, he's taking me up on my offer to truck the junk in his yard to the dump."

Kathy nodded. "I'm sure his neighbors will thank you. That property is a real eyesore."

"How's he been doing at The Bay Bar?"

Kathy shrugged. "Noreen hasn't complained, and all I care

about is that the tables are cleared before the next customers come in."

Tori nodded.

Just then, a knock came on the door and it opened. "Hey, girlfriends," Anissa called as she entered the kitchen.

"What's up?" Tori asked, taking in her friend's face, which could best be described as taut, her dark brown eyes shadowed with tension.

"Got any wine?" Anissa asked, already shucking her jacket and placing it on the back of one of the kitchen chairs before seating herself.

"The sun is barely over the yardarm," Kathy commented.

"Not hardly, and anyway, how could you tell with the gray skies we've been having?" Anissa asked.

Tori crossed over to the fridge and retrieved the open bottle of cheap red, grabbing two glasses from the cupboard and plunking them down on the scarred wooden table before pouring.

"Nothing for Kathy?" Anissa asked.

Kathy sighed. "I've got to be at work in ten minutes."

"So, how's the waitressing going?"

"I'm a server, not a waitress," Kathy said pointedly.

"Well, excuse me."

"You're excused," Kathy said with a smile.

Tori pushed the wine glass in Anissa's direction and took her usual seat at the table.

"I wouldn't want to be called a server. That title is a little too close to *servant* for me, and that's a little too close to slavery for this girl."

"Good point," Tori said.

"Well, it's gender-neutral, and I guess that's the descriptor of the day," Kathy said with a shrug.

"You liking the job?" Anissa asked.

Again, Kathy shrugged. "I'm thinking of investing in a pair of support hose. Standing for hours on end makes my legs feel like they're attached to lead weights."

Tori perked up. "Which reminds me of something Don Newton told me this morning."

"Well, put a pin in that thought because I've got to get over to the bar and start prepping for the evening's customers," Kathy said, crossed the kitchen, grabbed her jacket, and waved goodbye before heading out the door.

Tori glanced at Anissa. The women stared at each other for long seconds.

"What's wrong?" Tori asked.

Anissa's gaze dipped to the glass before her. She picked it up and gulped before setting it back on the table. "Detective Osborn —" she began.

Tori picked up her own glass and took a fortifying gulp in commiseration. Plunk went her glass on the table. "And?"

"He and some minions from the electric company were all over my house this morning, looking at all the electrical wires to see if they'd been messed with. See if anything was burned." She shook her head. "Seems like they can't wait to pin that Stanton man's death on me."

Did Tori dare to play devil's advocate?

She decided not to.

"Well, they didn't find anything, did they?"

"Damn right, they didn't," Anissa said fervently.

"Then you've got nothing to worry about."

"Says the little white gal," Anissa practically spat.

"Anissa," Tori chided.

The black woman's eyes filled with tears. "I'm sorry. It's not your fault that I've got a target on my back."

"If only whoever had dumped the body into one of my boats, it would be me they were looking at as a suspect."

"Yeah, and I appreciate that you gave me a free slip...too bad it's at the farthest spot away from the shop."

"If you like, I'll give you the top spot next season," Tori said sincerely.

Anissa shook her head. "I don't use the boat enough to warrant that, but I appreciate the offer."

No. Anissa had used her boat maybe four times during the entire season.

"I will not let them railroad you," Tori told her friend.

Anissa didn't look convinced. "Will you post my bail?"

"I'd put the entire compound on the line if those a-holes dare charge you."

Anissa's bottom lip quivered. "Thanks," she said, her voice husky.

"But it won't come to that because you've done nothing wrong."

"You're damn right I haven't. My only crime is being the only black face on Resort Road."

Tori was determined to think positively. "Osborn and the goonies found nothing on your property. Now they have to expand their territory to find out what actually happened to Chuck Stanton."

Anissa let out a breath. "I guess."

"No, think about it. Whatever happened to the dead guy, it had to be local. Nobody would lug a body miles away to dump it in one of the boats in my slips. And think about it. The guy's hand had to be clutching a high-voltage wire when he died. What circumstances would bring that into play?"

Anissa frowned. "Yeah, dying like that probably wasn't an act of aggression. But if the guy died by accident, why wouldn't someone just call nine-one-one and report it?"

Tori thought about it for a moment. "Because another crime had been perpetrated?"

Anissa looked skeptical. "I can't think of one. Can you?"

No. Tori had far too many thoughts whirling around her

mind. Her grandfather's arrival. Her lack of employment. The cost of renovating the boathouse.

She shook her head and took a sip of her crappy wine. She let her thoughts wander back on the day. "One of Don Newton's boats got loose this morning, and I took it back to him."

"And?" Anissa prodded.

"He knew the dead guy. Didn't think he was always on the up and up."

"In what way?"

"Possibly cheating during Don's sponsored fishing derbies. But the thing is, the dead guy never won. Just came in second."

"Cheated how?"

"He was suspected of shoving lead sinkers into the fish to make them weigh more. I'd say through the gills would be best, but what do I know about cheating in fishing derbies?"

"Sounds like a lot," Anissa remarked.

"My point is, if he was willing to cheat—or at least bend the rules—in one area of his life, why wouldn't he do it in others?"

"That's a pretty big leap in logic, isn't it?" Anissa asked.

Tori shrugged. "Maybe, maybe not."

Anissa looked thoughtful. "What could a guy like Stanton offer to people that was worth money?"

"Something under the table?" Tori asked.

Anissa looked doubtful.

"Yeah, I'm just spitballing here, but I can't shake the idea that Stanton died because of an accident, not murder," Tori reiterated.

"Yeah, well, the cops don't think so—else they wouldn't be harassing me."

Tori nodded in commiseration.

They sipped their wine in the deadly quiet kitchen, with only the grunts and groans of the old refrigerator interrupting the silence.

"Wanna keep me company for supper? I was gonna make mac and cheese."

"From a blue box?" Anissa asked warily.

"No. The gummy cheese kind."

Anissa grinned. "Sounds like heaven."

"It would be if Kathy was here to work her magic."

"Does Noreen feed her?"

"All the grease she can stand."

Anissa winced but then looked at the clock. "It's too early for supper."

Tori looked at her glass. "But not for another round."

Anissa smiled. "Girlfriend, you are speaking my language."

And they raised their glasses in salute.

CHAPTER 10

Tori decided to answer Eric's voice message that evening, texting him that she'd be available to load up the truck and take his discards to the dump at about eight the next morning. He texted back with a thumbs-up emoji.

As usual, this time of year, no customers were lining up to buy bait, so Tori hung up a sign that said BE BACK SOON and a little graphic of a clock where she could move the hands to say when she'd return. She set them to eleven o'clock, although she didn't think she'd be away that long. She threw her weed whacker into the back of her truck, pulled out of the lot, and headed north up Resort Road.

Tori parked her truck in front of the broken-down house. She tooted the horn, but there was no sign of Eric. This felt a little like when she and Kathy had helped Anissa clear out a decrepit house over on Falcon Island earlier that year, only this time, she was charged with clearing Eric's front yard—not the home's contents.

Eric had piled the assorted junk at the bottom of the yard. Empty red, plastic gas cans, cement blocks, plastic yard ornaments, rotting wood, and lichen-encrusted lawn furniture were piled chest-high. Another pile consisted of old metal objects, including a disassembled boat hoist, rusty bed springs, a battered barbeque grill, and goodness only knew what else.

Tori assumed the yard was clear of most detritus and retrieved the weed whacker from the back of her pickup. She revved up the powerful gas-driven motor and started hacking away at the more-than-foot-long grass. It wasn't long before a heavy-eyed Eric emerged from the home's front door and onto the sagging wooden porch. He waved to Tori, who shut down the whacker.

"Thanks for coming," Eric called.

Tori waved a hand in dismissal. "You wanna load up the back of the truck while I take care of this grass?"

"Sure thing," Eric replied and shambled down the steps. He tossed all the general trash into the back of the pickup, leaving the metal behind. Tori figured he'd want to make a separate run with that and turn it in for scrap value. That meant she'd be making two runs to the dump. Of course, she could just beg off on a second run, but she was sure Eric's neighbors would be glad to see the road's eyesore transform into a slightly lesser blight.

Tori had made a sizable dent clearing the front of the property by the time Eric loaded the last of the junk into the back of her pickup. Already, the property looked better. Then she realized she'd forgotten to ask Anissa the evening before if she'd loan Eric her mower. Well, they had a couple of months before the snow fell. She'd try to remember to speak to Anissa about it the next time they met.

Tori turned off the whacker and strode across the chopped grass to join Eric.

"Thanks for hacking down the meadow," he said and gave an embarrassed laugh.

"My pleasure." Tori pointed to a rusty old wheelbarrow beside the dwindling wood pile. "What about that?"

"It ain't broken. I use it in my garden."

Tori nodded. "We'd better get going."

"Sure thing," Eric said and followed Tori to the pickup, watching as she stowed the weed whacker on top of the junk, reining it in with a bungee cord.

They both got into the truck and fastened their seat belts. Tori started the engine, pulled into the neighbor's driveway, and turned the pickup around.

"I really appreciate all the help you've given me."

"You're welcome," Tori said. "Anything for Amber's friend."

She noted that Eric looked away, his gaze fixed on the landscape beyond the passenger window. "I haven't spoken to Amber in at least twenty years," Eric remarked.

"Well, you haven't missed much," Tori muttered.

Eric looked surprised. "I always thought you two got along fine."

"Never," Tori said succinctly.

Eric shrugged. "She could be a little bossy."

"Ha! That's putting it mildly. She's always been a bully." It was then Tori realized she'd said far too much. Still, the way her extended family treated her since Herb had sold her the compound for one dollar had been less than friendly and more like harassment. She didn't deserve to have the land and business. She had beguiled her grandfather into giving her the property that could be worth a million or more if it was developed—and that they, who had ignored Herb and Josie for years while they struggled to stay afloat, deserved a chunk of the spoils from Herb's lottery win.

Not really. Tori was glad she had the support of her grandfather, Kathy, and Anissa since she didn't feel she could trust her family—and especially her parents—to be in her corner. Sometimes, she wished she'd never have to put up with her parents ever again. But then, they'd made it pretty clear that they felt the same way about her. Okay, not so much her Dad, but he was cowed by his overbearing wife. More than once, Tori wondered how her cantankerous, opinionated grandfather had ever raised such a wimp. Or maybe it was that Tori's Gramps was just so strong that her father thought he could never measure up. Tori often felt sorry for her Dad and saw the sadness in his eyes when her mother berated her, but then he hadn't stood up to protect Tori from her mother's viperous attacks, either.

Tori turned on the radio so she and Eric wouldn't have to converse too much. The banter of the morning drive-time hosts was pretty innocuous, but it filled the conversational void in the truck's cab as Tori steered them to the county dump. They cleared the junk from the back of the pickup, and Eric asked about the scrap metal.

"If you take it to the reclamation site, I'll split the proceeds with you."

"You don't have to do that," Tori said. "I'm just glad to help a neighbor."

Eric beamed. "I'm glad to hear you say that. Are you handy when it comes to home repairs?"

His question was getting into territory Tori didn't want to explore. "Not really. I depend on—and pay for—Anissa Jackson's expertise."

"Oh. Yeah," Eric muttered meekly. Had he realized he was already in danger of abusing her goodwill? "Well, can we go to the scrap metal yard?"

Tori glanced at the dashboard's clock. "Yeah, but then I need to open the bait shop. I can't work for the school system with this black eye, so I need to make the shop pay ... if it can."

"Yeah, sure," Eric agreed.

They returned to Eric's yard. As they loaded up the scrap, Lucinda Bloomfield's vintage Town Car slowly passed by. Tori waved, and Lucinda raised a hand in acknowledgment, her expression one of gratitude. Tori and Lucinda, the mayor of Resort Road and the wealthiest woman in the county, weren't exactly friends, but they weren't exactly enemies, either. Lucinda liked things tidy. Eric's property was the lone remaining eyesore on Resort Road. It had to bring Lucinda unbridled joy to see it being cleaned up.

Tori and Eric finished loading the scrap and headed out once again.

Despite the radio's presence, the silence was strained until finally Eric broke the quiet to tell Tori how he cooked the fish he caught and the veggies he grew. Like her grandmother, Eric was canning his garden's tomatoes. He also had a chest freezer filled with zucchini, yellow squash, rhubarb, and three varieties of peppers.

"Are you a prepper?" Tori asked. Several of her customers were convinced the end of civilization was near and they were determined to be prepared to survive.

"Nah, I'm just broke. But now that I've got a job..." he said.

Tori frowned. Eric seemed to be counting an awful lot on the income from his minimum-wage job. But who was she to burst his bubble?

Eric collected the money for the metal and seemed pleased with the amount.

When they arrived back at his cottage, Eric reached for his wallet and pulled out a five-dollar bill. He shoved it in Tori's direction. "Thanks for all your help."

Tori shook her head. "Oh, no—you don't owe me anything."

"I do—if only for gas."

She took in his earnest expression and decided to take the offered bill if only to assuage Eric's sense of contrition.

"Thank you," Tori said.

Eric nodded, pleased. "Well, I guess I'll see you around."

"Count on it," Tori said.

Eric exited the truck and waited as Tori turned the pickup around and gave him a wave.

As the truck bumped along Resort Road, Tori wondered if that five dollars would be the only income she earned that day.

The kitchen had closed at The Bay Bar, and the last of the dinner guests had left when Kathy crossed her arms over her chest as she walked across the road. Threading her way through the shadows, Kathy made her way back to the Cannon bungalow, the place she now thought of as home. Pulling out her key, she opened the back door to the darkened kitchen. The lights were still on in the living room, so she knew that Tori had waited up for her.

"Hey, Tori," Kathy called.

"Hey, yourself."

Kathy found Tori had settled in Herb's old, creased, and cracked, brown faux-leather recliner with an afghan on her lap, surrounded by all three cats.

"Well, don't you look comfy," Kathy said, stripping off her sweater.

"I am, but boy, do I have to pee."

"Then go to the bathroom."

"And disturb the cats?"

Daisy, Henry, and Larry looked like it might take dynamite to loosen them from surrounding their human heating pad.

"Well, how'd dinner service go tonight?" Tori asked.

"The bar was hopping, but I only got to serve eight customers."

"Not worth the effort, then?"

"The effort, yeah. My time ... I'm not so sure."

"Are you going to quit?" Tori asked.

Kathy sighed. "I can't. I need what little money I'm making to stay afloat."

Tori nodded.

Kathy took a seat on the worn couch. "Want some wine?"

Tori shook her head. "I was waiting for you to come home,

and now I think I'll just head off to bed. Although, it's not like I need to get up early or anything."

Kathy took in Tori's face. The bruise under her eye wasn't quite as dramatic, but it was still pretty visible. "Did you hear from your grandfather?"

Tori shook her head and gestured toward her face. "I think Gramps is mad at me for this shiner."

"That's ridiculous. It wasn't like you wanted to get punched."

"Tell me about it," Tori muttered.

"There was a lot of talk about Chuck Stanton at the bar tonight."

"Oh, yeah?" Tori asked, sounding intrigued.

"Yeah. As I wasn't busy, Paul had me rolling cutlery in napkins for the next shift. I rolled way too many sets of flatware," she groused.

"Get to the juicy part," Tori encouraged.

Kathy shrugged. "I don't know that it was juicy, just guys swapping stories about their encounters with the guy."

"Give me a for instance," Tori said, stroking the back of Daisy's neck.

"It seems Chuck was a gambler—who was a heavy loser. The thing is, he always showed up to the next card game with a wad of cash. Bills that were well used."

Tori frowned. "Did anyone have a theory as to why those bills were so worn?"

"A theory," Kathy affirmed. "A couple of the guys wondered if he was shaking people down for the money."

Tori frowned. "By doing what?"

"That's the thing, nobody knew what."

"Sounds like idle speculation," Tori grumbled.

"Maybe," Kathy said.

"Anything else?"

"Seems he liked the ladies—and the younger, the better."

Tori frowned. "But his wife said—"

Kathy shrugged. "Cheaters gonna cheat. Some wives look the other way; some never know—or want to accept—the truth."

"Well, all I can say is that Alice Stanton wasn't faking it when she mourned for her dead husband. It was real, raw emotion she showed me, not an act."

"All I can tell you is what I heard. Apparently, Stanton was pretty close to one of The Bay Bar's waitresses for a while."

"And then what happened?" Tori asked.

"She left the area and was never heard from again."

"She's dead?" Tori asked incredulously.

"No, she moved to Rochester and got a job in a high-end restaurant."

"She didn't have his baby or anything scandalous?"

"Oh, Tor," Kathy said with pity, "having a baby out of wedlock hasn't been scandalous for quite a long time."

"Duh!" Tori acknowledged. "But it would be scandalous for his wife if it happened and word got around."

"Okay, I'll give you that," Kathy remarked.

Tori looked thoughtful. "Well, so far, we have a couple of reasons someone might have wanted to off the guy."

Kathy ticked off the items on her fingers. "Liar and cheat. Gambler who may or may not have owed someone big bucks—but I count that as a maybe, since he always seemed to have cash. And third, he might have knocked up a waitress, possibly abandoned her in her hour of need, and she—or someone else—was determined to make him pay."

"Nah, I don't believe that last one. If you want someone to pay, you hit them in the wallet, not knock them off."

"Maybe," Kathy agreed once more.

Tori looked thoughtful. "If Chuck Stanton showed up at the bar to flirt with one of the servers, then Paul must have known him. He had to be a good customer, right?"

"I suppose."

"Think you can ask him tomorrow night?"

"I'm not working tomorrow. And, anyway, how would I couch this info request?"

"Idle curiosity?" Tori suggested.

"I guess, but let's face it, if we weren't in the boonies, talk of the dead guy would have been over the day after his death."

"In case you don't remember, our friend Anissa seems to be the top suspect in the guy's death."

"Are you sure electrocution can be considered murder?" Kathy asked.

"Moving the body away from the accident site sure can be construed as a crime."

Kathy nodded. "Yeah, I guess you're right."

"And we—or at least I—care that Anissa might be in trouble."

"Are you insinuating that I don't care what happens to her? She's my friend, too," Kathy asserted.

"Yeah, but she and I have a long history," Tori countered.

"A history with a very long interruption," Kathy reminded her friend.

"Even so," Tori began, "I'm not going to let anyone railroad her into some kind of wrongful death scenario."

"I wouldn't, either," Kathy said defensively.

"Good," Tori said definitively.

Daisy stood up, stretching her front legs and then her back before jumping down to the carpet. As soon as she did, Kathy's boys followed suit. Tori pushed the chair into its full upright position.

"Did Anissa drop by?" Kathy asked.

Tori shook her head. "I was hoping she would. It gets lonely around here when you're gone."

"Aw," Kathy simpered. "You *do* love me."

Tori laughed. "Of course I do. And I miss your cooking even more."

Not exactly what Kathy wanted to hear, but she knew where her roommate was coming from.

"What are your plans for tomorrow?" Kathy asked.

"I'm not sure. If nothing else, I can sit in the shop all day making pendants and earrings for my Etsy shop. Christmas is coming," she reminded Kathy.

Yeah, and she had no intention of opening her inn for the holiday itself. But she could offer dates up to the big day. And unfortunately, she had to host Noreen's sister-in-law's bridal shower in two days—and it was not something she was looking forward to.

Tori rose from her chair. "I've got to pee before I explode."

"Well, if you do it here, I'm not gonna clean it up," Kathy said in jest. Then again, she was deadly serious.

Tori tottered off in the direction of the bathroom, and Kathy grabbed her sweater, turned off the lights in the living room, and headed for her bedroom. When she got there, she found both her boys sitting on the bottom of the bed waiting for her. "You know I've got to read for at least half an hour before I turn out the light," she warned them. Larry turned his back on her, sauntered up the bed, and hunkered down in front of her pillows. "You're going to have to move," she warned the cat. If the cat could have taunted her, he would have, and she knew she would sidle in as best she could so as not to disturb the boy. She was a sucker that way...as were most true cat lovers. Why such small creatures held sway over their owners was a mystery to Kathy but one she wasn't inclined to try and solve.

Kathy changed into her PJs and slid onto the mattress, trying not to disturb her cats. She grabbed her current read but didn't open the book. She'd been working at The Bay Bar for almost a week and acknowledged that she'd begun to hate the sight of the place. The odor of charred burgers and greasy fries was starting to make her cringe. Kathy swallowed, realizing she could not work as a server for the entire winter. Somehow, she would have to find a way for Swans Nest to pay for itself over the long, snowy winter.

Okay, she had at least seven weekends to fill before Thanksgiving. She could advertise in the local Penny Saver, but that audience wasn't really her demographic. Maybe she should step up her posts on social media. She could do that. Maybe she and Tori could work together on that, as Tori was in the same financial bind. Updating her website was another option. Then it occurred to her that she could list the place with short-term vacation rental platforms. Such places took a hefty cut, but also offered protection against unruly guests. Even with a cut in profits, Swans Nest would still be in business. Maybe.

Who'd want to escape to the boonies in the dead of winter? Crazy people? People who just wanted a respite? She had three guest rooms. Maybe she could offer the place as a writer's or artist's retreat?

Kathy set the book aside, slipped out of bed, and headed for the darkened office she shared with Tori to grab a yellow tablet of paper. She intended to write down all her ideas, type them up in the morning, and do some online research.

She was determined to make Swans Nest a success.

She really had no other option.

CHAPTER 11

Once again, Tori got up before Kathy. She had a solitary breakfast and retreated to the bait shop to work on her broken china jewelry. Tori examined the bruise around her eye. It was beginning to fade. She knew it would turn yellow just before it disappeared. That couldn't happen soon enough. On a good day, she could churn out seven to ten pieces. She'd take pictures, upload them to her Etsy shop, and cross her fingers that they'd sell. Sometimes, she posted them on the shop's social media pages, but it was mostly men who visited those sites. Still, she'd added a category that said, "Treat your honey to...."

Was it a good idea or just desperation?

This led her to her next thought.... Her grandfather hadn't contacted her or returned to the compound since Tuesday. He was the only family member she felt she could count on, and now, was he ghosting her because some punk had used her as a punching bag? That wasn't fair but she knew it was the way Herb looked at things.

Tori had completed one pendant and began work on another when the shop's door opened. Still dressed in her pajamas, Kathy appeared swathed in her jacket and holding a mug. "I thought I'd find you here. I brought you a hot mug of tea fixed just the way you like it."

"Aw, thanks," Tori said, gratefully accepting the offering. "What's up?"

Kathy let out a breath. "I've decided I can't let Swans Nest sit empty most of the winter. I'm going to list it on the online marketplaces for short-term rentals."

"I thought you didn't want to do that," Tori remarked.

"There're a lot of things I don't want to do—like play waitress all winter."

Tori nodded. "It sucks being broke."

"Tell me about it. But I was thinking.... You've got your furniture fund for the boathouse reno."

"I'm not touching that," Tori said fervently.

"Hear me out. I don't have to work tonight. I was thinking that it might be fun to go to the auction house in Warton to look at what's on offer at their weekly sale. We haven't gone in forever."

No, not since Kathy was furnishing Swans Nest.

Tori raised an eyebrow. "I suppose we could."

"I mean, you wouldn't have to buy anything. Just look."

"Yeah. We know how that works out," Tori said sourly.

Kathy shrugged. "If nothing else, you might get a project piece you can work on over the winter."

"That's true." Tori thought about it. She had nothing better to do in the evenings. Okay, let's go. Do you think Anissa might want to come along?"

"We can but ask."

Tori nodded. "I'll text her."

"Great."

Tori sipped her tea.

"Have you heard from Herb?" Kathy asked.

"Nope," Tori said succinctly.

"We could invite him and Irene to dinner on Sunday. We can do it at the house or at Swans Nest. What do you think?"

"Sunday is the baby shower," Tori said.

"I'm sure he won't want to go to that. Maybe we could invite him to lunch? We could invite Anissa, too, and she could fill him in on everything that's left to do at The Lotus Lodge."

It sounded like a good idea. "I could call him this morning. I could also ask him to come and visit before then, too."

"And what if he won't come?" Kathy asked, her voice subdued.

"Then I guess I'm skunked." Tori's lip trembled. "I don't understand why Gramps blames *me* for getting hurt at school."

"He blamed you when you lost your teaching job in the suburbs, too, even though it was the school system that was cutting jobs—not anything anybody did."

"Yeah," Tori said, her voice clipped.

"Why don't you invite him to come with us to the auction tonight?"

Tori shook her head. "I'm sure he'd just think I was trying to get him to buy something for either the boathouse or The Lotus Lodge."

"So what? He offered to pay for the upgrades to the lodge."

"But not the furnishings."

"And you would never ask him to do so."

Tori wasn't convinced.

"Look at it this way: I'm betting Herb is bored silly with all the baby shower talk. By tonight, he'll be willing to set fire to his boots just for a break from it all."

Tori almost smiled. That sounded about right. "Okay. But don't count on him accepting either invitation."

"He can do what he wants. Making the offer is a kind of peace offering—not that you've done anything wrong."

Yeah. She hadn't.

"Okay. I'll do that. And if he declines, I'll wait until Saturday to invite him for lunch on Sunday. If he declines my invitation, I'm sure there'll be leftovers at the baby shower."

"Don't be such a pessimist," Kathy admonished.

"I've known Gramps a lot longer than you have," Tori said sadly.

"Yeah, well, sometimes people change."

"And more often, they don't," Tori countered.

"Your grandfather loves you," Kathy asserted. "He's just stubborn."

"I'll say." Tori decided to change the subject. "What do you have to do to get Swans Nest ready for Noreen's party tomorrow? Do you need help serving?"

Kathy shook her head. "Didn't I tell you? I don't have to do a damn thing."

"What?" Tori asked, confused.

"Noreen's just paying for the venue. She's in charge of the catering and the decorations."

"How's she going to do all that and run the bar for the lunch and dinner crowd?"

"Not my problem," Kathy said. "She made it clear she just wanted to book the parlor only—and for peanuts. I'm really surprised at her. She knows what dire straits I'm in. She knows what it takes to keep a business in the black."

"You could have said no," Tori pointed out.

"And make an enemy of my next-door neighbor? I don't think so," Kathy asserted.

"I'm sorry to hear that. And it sounds like Noreen is stretching herself far too thin."

"That's not my problem," Kathy reiterated. She didn't sound pleased.

Tori nodded.

Kathy wrapped her arms around her chest. "I'm cold. Don't you ever turn the heat up in here?"

"Not past sixty. That'll feel like heaven come winter."

"Yeah, well, it's not winter."

"And I'm out of work for at least another week," Tori pointed out.

"Oh, yeah. I'm sorry." Kathy said. "Well, I'm going in to change into something a lot warmer. Then I'm going across the street to Swans Nest to give the parlor a good vacuum and dusting so it's ready for tomorrow."

"Go you," Tori cheered.

Kathy nodded, turned, and exited the bait shop.

Tori watched her disappear from sight before looking at the clock. It was after eight. Her grandfather used to wake up at the crack of dawn. Now that he was retired, had he changed his habits? Was it too early to give him a call?

Tori decided to risk it.

Consulting the contacts list on her phone, she tapped Herb's name. As expected, the call went to voice mail. "Hey, Gramps, Kathy and I are going to the Warton auction house tonight—just to see what's available. We'd love to have you join us. Call me back and let me know. Love you," Tori said and ended the message.

Well, it was now up to Herb to respond. Would he give her a yay or a nay?

She'd just have to wait to find out.

~

THE JOY KATHY felt when walking into Swans Nest never ceased to amaze her. Although she'd only spent a few nights in the B&B, testing the rooms, it felt like home to Kathy. She'd been involved in every aspect of the renovation and had learned to do things like sand drywall, paint, and do minor repairs, all under Anissa's tutelage. She knew how to snake a plugged toilet or sink and other simple home repairs. But what she loved most about hosting people and parties was the cooking. She didn't have to do that for Noreen's sister-in-law's bridal shower. She didn't have to provide food or drink, and she didn't have to decorate. Still, if there was one thing Kathy also loved to do, it *was* to decorate. She decorated for even the slightest of holidays. Right then, her theme was autumn, with faux pumpkins, leaves, and sunflowers. Her guests seemed to like it.

Always a bridesmaid, never a bride, Kathy thought. Well, she'd actually only been a bridesmaid once at her brother's wedding. She'd thought Chelsea and her might become best buddies, but even before the wedding, it became obvious that it wasn't going to happen. Chelsea was jealous of the relationship Kathy had with her brother and had succeeded in eroding it, much to Kathy's chagrin. The woman had been so bold as to tell Kathy that her brother "doesn't need you. He's got *me*." Yes, that about said it all. Kathy hadn't said anything to Danny. What good would it have done except to force the wedge Chelsea had driven between them even wider? She'd done the same with their parents, insisting that holidays be spent with her family. Kathy had a feeling that when (if) they had children, Chelsea would keep the Grant family at arm's length and that Dan would let her have her way. It was always easier to acquiesce than to fight.

Coward, she thought, though she'd never voice that opinion in polite company.

Still, Kathy loved to throw a good party—and that included decorating—so it wasn't a surprise that she felt the need to check out the decorations she'd accumulated for bridal showers. After hosting afternoon tea, it was her favorite kind of event to host.

Tucking her phone into her slacks pocket, Kathy descended the stairs to her basement and the small storeroom which served as a holding place for decorations, paper supplies, and an auxiliary pantry for canned and other goods sealed against vermin and other pests.

Kathy pulled out the box of things left behind after the bridal showers she'd hosted over the summer. There'd been four of them, and at every one, there'd been something left behind that she might use should she have to decorate for such an occasion. Noreen had said she didn't need to supply anything, but Kathy liked to check on her party inventory from time to time...just because.

Kathy had totes stored in the attic for all sorts of occasions. She'd collected quite a few Christmas decorations but also had begun to collect things for the other holidays of the year: Easter, Mother's Day, wedding and baby showers, patriotic stuff that could be used for Memorial Day, Fourth of July, and Labor Day, autumn, Halloween, and Thanksgiving. Most of it had come from thrift shops and yard sales, but it was all good stuff that she would use again and again when circumstances demanded it.

Kathy opened the plastic tote containing the bridal shower items: a satin sash that said "Bride-to-Be," white crepe streamers, white balloons, two white-tissue fold-out wedding bells, a tiara, paper plates that said Mr. & Mrs., various decorated napkins, a banner stating "Happily Ever After," etc.

Replacing the lid on the tote, Kathy inspected her yard and thrift shop autumn finds. It puzzled her how people gave up such pretty items for a song just to change things out. Their loss, her gain. She wasn't going to go through her Christmas stuff, but this was the first season she'd be able to decorate Swans Nest for the holidays. She had a nicely shaped tree she'd found at a yard sale for $30. It was a little pricy for such a venue, but if she got ten years out of the tree, it would only cost her $3 a year. Depreciation was her friend. Some of the baubles were vintage, but she'd have to buy more. She could string popcorn and cranberries. The popcorn would last the season. She wasn't sure about the cranberries. Still, if they shriveled up, she could craft a new string. She'd think about it. An old-fashioned tree would look so pretty in the parlor.

As she packed the things away, she made a mental note to jot down her ideas for what she needed. Maybe she could find discounted baubles on Facebook Marketplace or at the local church-run thrift shops. Their prices were usually pretty good. And there were still a couple of rummage sales to be held before the end of October. She still had time.

Replacing the totes in her basement storage space, Kathy headed upstairs.

Drawn to the parlor, Kathy inspected the room. She might have to bring up some folding chairs for the Saturday bridal shower. She'd vacuum and dust but if she wasn't expected to decorate or provide anything to eat, she'd just stand by in the kitchen in case a light bulb blew or if they ran out of plastic cups. She could sit at the kitchen island and work on her plans to promote Swans Nest.

One more shift, Kathy told herself. *One more shift,* and then she'd get three days off. She'd added up her tips from the six nights she'd worked, which amounted to just over three hundred dollars. But she figured if she'd been working a minimum-wage job, she'd probably have made just as much, if not more, with a lot less hassle. Not being able to work on the weekends would mean that her tips would be even less the next week. The Bay Bar paid the minimum wage for servers—which was far less than regular workers. Hadn't Tori said Herb told her about an opening at Tom's Grocery in Warton? She wondered if the job had already been filled. Of course, traveling into the village would cost her gas, but it might be worth it—at least until the snow fell and the roads were treacherous.

So many thoughts circled her brain as she tidied the already immaculate space. What she wanted was to stay put, to have people travel to her, and for her to make their stay cozy, warm, and fun.

With nothing else to do, Kathy turned down the heat, locked the front door behind her, and returned to the Cannon bungalow. She would dig through the wheezing old refrigerator's freezer, find something to use as a jumping point for dinner, and make enough to feed herself and Tori—and maybe Anissa—and maybe do laundry before her lunch shift at The Bay Bar. And she'd noodle on what needed to be done to lure guests to Swans Nest.

For some silly reason, Kathy had a feeling she could make her inn pay for itself during the long, cold winter.

She just had to.

CHAPTER 12

After reaching her jewelry-making goal for the day, Tori set up her lights in the bait shop. Although it looked pretty professional, she'd gotten the lights for a song from an online sale. YouTube videos taught her how to use them. As she hadn't had a customer all day, she figured she wasn't likely to be disturbed by selling worms or minnows.

She screwed her phone onto the tripod, adjusted the angle of the umbrellas, and took pictures of her latest broken-china pendants, earrings, and rings. They looked *good*. Pretty. Hopefully, some—all?—of them would make it under scores of Christmas trees or in stockings hung from fireplace mantels this holiday season and their recipients would gush over and love the fruits of her labor.

She was just about to snap a last photo when her phone rang, startling her. Being screwed to the tripod, she had a devil of a time answering the call.

"Gramps? Is that you?"

"Of course, it's me. Who did you expect?"

The school district. Kathy. Anissa. The man in the moon.

"What's up?"

"So, Irene's been having me cart her around the county from Timbuktu to the moon since we got here."

"Is that because it's only your name on the rental form?"

"Yeah. I ain't about to buck their rules and get in trouble, so I been kinda busy."

Okay.

"But I think I can get away tonight to go to the auction house. I'm bettin' a load of my customers will be there, and it would be nice to catch up."

"Great."

"What time you going?"

"Uh, we haven't pinned that down yet. I'm still waiting to hear from Anissa."

"Okay. Text me with the particulars."

"You got it." Tori paused. "I'm glad we'll be able to spend some time together."

"We can spend all day Sunday together. Ain't no way I'm going to that baby shower."

Tori laughed. "Great. I'll be in touch. Love you, Gramps."

"And I love you, too, Tori."

～

DURING THE PRECEDING DAYS, Noreen hadn't mentioned plans for the wedding shower that would happen the next day, which made Kathy feel uncomfortable. Okay, she was only supposed to provide the venue and at a cut-rate price but not doing anything felt wrong. Kathy was determined to pin down her new boss for details since she wouldn't be working that evening and have another opportunity to speak with Noreen before the shower. She figured she ought to do it before her afternoon shift ended.

Kathy grabbed her jacket grom a peg in the entryway. Paul was already behind the bar and called out to her. "Not a bad crowd, huh?"

"Yeah. Before I go, I need to talk to Noreen about the wedding shower tomorrow."

"My sister is so excited," Paul said with a grin. "She's got people coming in from Rochester, Batavia, and a couple from Buffalo that she hasn't seen in a while. It should be a good time for all."

"I sure hope so," Kathy said, but something niggled in the back of her mind. "Noreen said there could be as many as fifteen guests."

Paul beamed. "Maybe twenty."

Kathy sank onto one of the bar stools. "Twenty?" She'd have to make sure both her parlors were ready for that number of guests. Of course, she could set up the buffet of whatever Noreen brought over in the dining room, and everyone could either eat at the breakfast tables where Kathy hosted her B&B guests or they could sit and snack in the parlors—which meant that something would get spilled and/or ground into the carpet. Thankfully, she had a steam cleaner that did a pretty good job in those circumstances.

"Noreen!" Paul called. "Kathy wants to talk about the shower."

They waited in silence for long seconds before Paul volunteered, "I'd better go get her," and left the bar, heading for the kitchen.

More time passed and Kathy was starting to feel antsy when Noreen emerged from the kitchen and strode to the bar. "You wanted to see me?" she asked, clipping her words.

Kathy cleared her throat and plastered on a smile. "I was thinking we ought to finalize plans for the shower."

Noreen frowned. "Don't worry, I've got everything covered."

Kathy wasn't convinced. "Everything?"

"Yes, everything," Noreen said with a touch of impatience.

Kathy nodded. "What time did you want to start setting up?"

Noreen shrugged. "Around one."

Kathy frowned. "But the shower is supposed to start at two."

"Look, this isn't rocket science."

"Yes, but—"

"Sorry, but I gotta prep for the onslaught," Noreen said and strode away.

"Okay," Kathy called after her, but her feeling of discomfort only increased. Something about the set of Noreen's jaw and her body language seemed off. Kathy was determined to find out just what that meant.

It had been a week since she started working at The Bay Bar. The tips were good, but was she going to get a paycheck anytime soon? When Paul returned, she asked the question.

"Oh, Noreen does the payroll over the weekend. We'll have a check ready for you on Monday. Sound good?"

Not really. She'd worked the previous Friday, Saturday, and Sunday. Shouldn't she have been paid on Monday for those hours? Apparently, it was what it was.

Kathy forced a smile. "Sure. See ya."

The chilly air seemed like a slap in the face. This was nothing to what it would be like in February. The idea of waiting tables until spring filled her with despair.

I can't do this. I can't do this until May.

There was only one shred of hope. Her marketing plan for Swans Nest. It had to work. It just had to.

CHAPTER 13

Just after four, Tori closed the bait shop, locked the door, and headed for the bungalow. She found Kathy sitting at the kitchen table with a yellow pad filled with scribbled notes.

"Plotting the takeover of the planet?" she asked, setting her box of jewelry down and hanging up her coat.

Kathy looked up. "Don't I wish. Instead, I called Katie Bonner."

Tori's eyes widened in delight. "How's she doing?"

"That girl's on her way to owning half of McKinlay Mill. I asked if I could pick her brain for promotional tips."

It helped to have a friend with a master's degree in marketing. "And?" Tori pressed.

"You know she always wanted to own a B&B. She's got a whole portfolio of ideas she's willing to share. She's going to email it to me, and since Monday is her day off, we're going to do an online meeting."

Tori leaned against the counter. "Can I sit in on the call? Not just to chat, but maybe she'll have some ideas for me, too."

"You know she'd love to talk to you, too," Kathy said. It had been too long since Kathy had sounded so happy.

"Boy, am I looking forward to Monday," Tori said, but then she remembered that her Gramps would be leaving that day, too. Talking to Katie would only help to lift her spirits.

And, thinking about her grandfather....

"I heard from Gramps. He sounded relieved to get a reprieve from talk of babies and Irene's family. He's hoping to meet up with some of his old customers at the auction tonight."

Kathy was tight-lipped but said nothing, apparently still smarting over Herb wanting to stay for free at Swans Nest on a future visit. Of course, there was the possibility that Tori could pay Kathy for Herb's and Irene's stay at the inn, or maybe she could barter something of equal value. Of course, Kathy might remember that she'd lived rent-free for over a year at the bungalow, but Tori wasn't going to mention that. Kathy pulled her weight with most of the cooking and cleaning—so much so that, at times, Tori actually felt guilty.

"Irene's got Gramps so booked up, it looks like I'm only going to see him tonight and Sunday. They go back to Florida on Monday afternoon. I was thinking maybe I could cook a chicken or something for him on Sunday when he comes to spend the afternoon."

"You roast a chicken? And what would you serve with it?" Kathy asked with skepticism.

"We've got frozen veggies. Corn. Mixed vegetables."

"Your grandfather likes stuffing. Do you know how to make it?"

"Uh, well, no. But I'm sure I could learn. I can visit Tom's Grocery in Warton tomorrow to get everything I need."

Kathy nodded. Was she waiting for Tori to beg her to help with the meal? No, that wasn't Kathy's style.

"I'm sure you'll do fine," Kathy said kindly. "Yell if you need help."

"Don't worry. I will."

Tori leaned against the counter. "What else have you been up to all day?"

Kathy looked distinctly unhappy. "After my shift, I spoke to Noreen asking for details about the party."

"And?"

"She got annoyed."

Tori frowned. "Are you just going to turn your place over to her?"

"Not a chance. I'll be there the whole time. I can read or do something else in the kitchen. I don't intend to hover, but I'm not leaving the premises just in case there's an accident or something."

"Good idea."

"And what will you do until Herb shows up this evening?"

Tori shrugged. "Inventorying and boxing the jewelry I've made over the past few days and hope like hell they sell this holiday season."

Kathy toyed with the pen that sat before her. "I should find a hobby that pays, too."

"So far, I've only broken even. Christmas is make-it or break-it time."

"What if it breaks you?"

Tori frowned, her gaze dipping to take in the floor. "Then I don't know what I'll do. After what happened on Monday, I'm worried the school district won't let me teach anymore. I suppose I could put in applications in the surrounding districts, but the idea of commuting in lake-effect snow squalls gives me the willies."

"I admit it; I wasn't prepared for how bad the weather could be on the bay, but honestly, I wouldn't want to live anywhere else," Kathy said.

Her words touched Tori's heart as she felt the same way, although she didn't say so. Some things didn't need to be said.

Tori pushed away from the counter. "Shall I invite Gramps and Anissa to have supper with us before we go to the auction?"

"Sure. I'm sure I can stretch supper to feed one more."

"Thanks, Kath. You're a doll."

"Yeah? Barbie or one of those Brats?"

Tori laughed. "Definitely a Brat."

"I'll take that as a compliment," Kathy said, got up, and cleared the notes from the table. "I thought we might have tacos tonight?" she suggested. "They're one of Anissa's favorites. If the idea of going to the auction doesn't entice her, my tacos will."

"I'll be sure to mention it to her," Tori said,

Tori spent the next few minutes texting her grandfather and Anissa, the latter of whom was the first to answer.

Is the pope catholic?

Her grandfather answered the text several hours later. *Having dinner with Irene's family, but will be at the compound before seven.*

That was cutting things close, as the pre-view time started at 6:30, and the auction began at 7:15 sharp. Well, it was what it was, and she only had to kill a few hours before the highlight of her day.

Great. Just great.

∼

ANISSA SHOWED up at her usual time, bringing a bag of tortilla chips and a jar of salsa as an appetizer. Since they didn't have any tequila for margaritas, they toasted each other with flat ginger ale, ate supper, and waited for Herb to arrive.

Tori and her grandfather headed for the auction house in Tori's truck while Kathy rode shotgun with Anissa. The parking lot was crowded, as it always was on a Friday night, and the aroma of grilled hamburgers and popcorn hung heavy in the air.

"I'm gonna get me some of that popcorn. I haven't had movie-style popcorn in ages," Anissa said.

"You had it when we went to the movies in Warton last month," Kathy pointed out.

"Yeah, and that was *ages* ago," Anissa said and laughed.

"I just made some the other night," Tori protested.

"Yes, but it wasn't greasy *movie* popcorn."

"Well, I'm full from supper," Tori said. "How about you, Gramps?"

"I might have me a burger. Irene's people are eating healthy. There's only so much skinless, grilled chicken a man can stomach."

Tori stifled a smile.

They entered the building and headed for the rows of items on offer that night. Herb and Anissa made a beeline for the tools, and Tori and Kathy went straight to the furniture section.

"What are you looking for?" Tori asked Kathy.

"Nothing special, although I'm thinking ahead for when Anissa can get started on my attic suite, hopefully next year ... *if* I have a good summer, that is." Kathy had hoped that work could start during the offseason. Still, there was no harm in planning ahead, and if she bought something, she could store it in the attic until it could be used.

"Is that tip money you made this past week burning a hole in your wallet?" Tori asked.

"Not exactly. I've still got the utility bill to pay at the end of the month, but I might be able to stretch a little to buy something small—like a hand mirror for the top of a dresser," she said sarcastically.

"Goals are goals."

"What do you want to find?"

"I like your suggestion of a refinishing project. Something useful that's kinda beat up but that I could make pretty."

It seemed that most of the furniture on offer that night was of the beat-up variety: dressers of maple and oak, chairs with sagging seats and moth-eaten upholstery, and a cherry secretary with a lot of water damage. You name it, someone had abused it. Kathy was drawn to a Victoria bedroom suite. The bed was too small, for modern-day comfort, but she knew Anissa could convert it to fit a queen-sized mattress.

"Would you paint it?" Tori asked.

"Hell, no. It's beautiful the way it is...or how it *could* be when refinished."

"Looks granny chic to me."

"And isn't that the point of an old-fashioned inn?" Kathy asked.

Tori wasn't about to offer a reply to that rhetorical question. Her taste in furnishings leaned toward contemporary—with an emphasis on comfort. That said, the furnishings at the bungalow were strictly hand-me-downs and chipboard. Once she got the boathouse and Lotus Lodge up and running—and paying for themselves—she could then concentrate on updating the bungalow. In the meantime, maybe she'd invest in a bigger dresser. The one she had now was too small and she kept half of her clothes in a laundry basket at the bottom of her closet.

Kathy had moved on to the box lots when Anissa joined Tori, with a popcorn bag in hand. She offered it to Tori.

"No, thanks. It smells great, but I'm still full from supper."

"Suit yourself."

"No good tools?"

Anissa shrugged. "There's a planer that looks interesting. Too bad I don't have anywhere to store it. It just reminds me that I need to build me a garage and workshop. I could do a lot of fun projects if I had a real workshop."

"Can you afford it?"

Anissa's lips curved into a smile. "Just about."

"That's great," Tori said, wondering if such a project would put hers or Kathy's renovations on the back burner. "Anything else interesting?" Tori asked, noticing her grandfather was handling some kind of tool.

"Nah, everything's either junk or cruddy with grease. My tools *never* look like that." Anissa nodded at the dresser that stood before them. "You thinking of buying that thing?"

"I am. Kathy thinks I need a project to refinish."

Anissa stepped forward and flicked a chip of paint off the top. "Looks like oak underneath, but are you sure it's your style? Looks like it's at least a hundred years old."

"It's bigger than what I've got. If I can get it cheap enough, I can make it work."

"Uh-huh." Anissa looked around, zeroing in on where a group of men were examining the fishing gear on offer. "I've been thinking of getting a new casting reel. I wonder if I could get one cheap but better than what I've got."

"Let's take a look," Tori said.

It seemed like Herb had the same idea, for he was also heading in that direction.

The women had to inch their way past the guys, who were examining the poles and other equipment, and Anissa was drawn to a table with the reels, wicker creels, and tackle boxes. Tori had inherited her grandfather's fishing gear and sold some in her shop, so she didn't see much of interest, although it all seemed to be in good shape. Whoever had owned it had taken care of his equipment.

While Anissa studied the reels, Tori's gaze wandered, and she was surprised to see Alice Stanton in the auction house's small café, looking forlorn as she sat at one of the tables with a Styrofoam cup in front of her.

Tori nudged Anissa. "I think I'll get some hot chocolate. Be back in a flash."

Anissa barely seemed to hear her.

Tori walked up to the counter, bought a cup of cocoa, and approached the small table. "Is this seat taken?"

Alice looked up. She seemed to have gained a lot more fine lines around her eyes during the days since they'd first met. The skin under her eyes was dark—perhaps from lack of sleep, or more likely that she'd been crying. "No."

Tori pulled the battered folding metal chair back and sat down. Dang—these things were always cold! She removed the plastic cap from her cup and took a tentative sip. Yikes—too hot. "I was surprised to see you here. Are you looking for something special?"

Alice shook her head. "I'm selling some of Chuck's fishing gear."

Tori's eyes widened. "Yeah, I was just looking at what's going up tonight. He had some good stuff."

Alice gave a snort of a laugh. "I gave him a lot of it for birthdays and Christmases. He loved it all."

"I take it you don't fish."

Alice shook her head. She looked awfully sad and Tori struggled to come up with a cheerful subject but couldn't. "How are you getting on?"

"Not well," Alice remarked. "Chuck dying was such a shock. But then…." She looked into Tori's eyes and seemed to make a decision. "You'd think after living with someone for almost twenty-seven years, you'd know everything about them."

Uh-oh. It sounded like Alice had only just found out about her husband's gambling addiction.

"Financial problems?" Tori guessed.

Alice nodded. "I'm probably going to have to sell my home. I've already sold Chuck's vehicles, and I've spoken to Bud here at the auction house about taking most of the contents of the house."

"Gee, I'm sorry to hear that."

"It's not going to be enough," Alice said sadly. "I was going to give Chuck a good sendoff, but I had to go with the cheapest cremation package the funeral home offered. I even had to call off the wake…." She shook her head and whispered. "How could he leave me like this?"

Did she mean to leave her by dying or leave her in monetary ruin?

Having to quickly liquidate her assets could only mean one thing. Tori hesitated before asking her next question. "Have you been threatened by anyone?"

Alice's head jerked up, her eyes wild. "Why would you ask that?"

Her reaction said it all.

Tori changed tacks. "Have you heard from Detective Osborn?"

Alice shook her head.

"I think you should call him. He may be able to help you with … with some of your problems."

"I don't see how."

"Cops have their ways," Tori said obliquely.

"I couldn't call. They watch me. Maybe I'm paranoid, but I think my phone's been tapped, too."

Tori nodded. "Would you like me to speak with the detective?"

Alice gave the barest of nods.

"Would you prefer to speak with him at his office so that the watchers can't listen in?"

Again, Alice nodded.

"Okay."

A rumble in the crowd caused the women to look over to the podium with a microphone where the beefy auctioneer was preparing for his night's work.

"Chuck's gear is supposed to be the third lot up," Alice said.

Tori nodded. "When you're ready to leave, would you like me to walk you to your car—in case someone is waiting for you?"

Alice let out a breath. "Yes, thank you. But then, I've got nobody to walk me into the house once I get home."

"Would you like me to follow you home?"

Tears welled in Alice's eyes, and she whispered, "Yes, please."

Tori nodded.

"I can wait until you're done with your business. Goodness knows I've got nothing else to do in the evenings anymore," Alice said.

"I'm so sorry for your troubles," Tori said sincerely.

"Yeah, me, too," Alice muttered.

Tori picked up her untouched chocolate and got up. "Stay here. I'll go tell my friends what's what, and we'll figure something out."

"Thank you."

"You bet," Tori said, giving the woman a wan smile.

As she walked across the cavernous room, Tori wondered how her grandfather was going to react to the news she was taking on another lost soul. Would it be pride or anger?

She'd just have to wait to find out.

CHAPTER 14

Kathy and Anissa were only too happy to help out Alice Stanton by acting as escorts to her home, making sure she entered her house without incident. According to Tori, Herb was tight-lipped during the drive. "You shoulda just called the deputies," he kept muttering.

After Herb left, Kathy listened as Tori left a detailed message for Detective Osborn, who returned her call early the next morning. Early enough to awaken Kathy, who tended to sleep in later than her roommate.

Tori gave her the lowdown as Kathy made a pot of coffee for herself and then ate a hardboiled egg with a slice of toast. Tori planned to work on jewelry in her ersatz studio, crossing her fingers to have a few bait customers. Meanwhile, Kathy did a load of laundry before heading over to Swans Nest to make sure everything was ready for the bridal shower.

Paul arrived at Swans nest just after eleven, since the front door was unlocked, he knocked before letting himself in.

"Hey, Kath! You here?"

Kathy hurried out of the kitchen to meet him in the hallway, still wiping her wet hands on a dishtowel. "Hey, Paul, what's up?"

She'd been expecting Noreen to show up.

"I brought over the cake for the shower." He held out a plastic-domed cake that had obviously come from Tom's Grocery in Warton.

"Seems a little small for the crowd that's coming this afternoon," Kathy commented.

"Yeah, but I'm sure you're going to put on a great spread for the guests."

Kathy felt her heart sink. "Me?"

"Yeah, you're practically famous around here for these kinds of parties. I thought I might pop over later to take some pictures if I can get one of the servers to mind the bar for a few minutes."

Kathy hesitated. "Noreen said—"

"Yeah, that all she had to bring was this cake. It's swell of you to take care of everything else."

Really?

Kathy decided not to deliver the bad news to him.

"I was kind of surprised Noreen volunteered to throw the shower," Paul remarked.

"Oh?"

"Yeah, she and my sister have clashed before, but that's all water under the bridge."

Kathy nodded. "I take it you and your sister are close."

"Yeah." He laughed. "Sometimes, Noreen gets jealous that we talk almost every day. You've got a brother. Don't you talk often?"

No, they didn't. Not that Kathy wanted it that way, but her brother was in a relationship and.... Sometimes women weren't nice to each other, something Kathy could never fathom.

"You want your sister to have a great shower, don't you?" Kathy asked.

"Of course. She's had it rough. Her husband was killed in a motorcycle accident seven years ago. She was devastated. I'm happy she's found someone else and that he's a great guy."

"Does he ride?"

"No," Paul said emphatically. "Barb wasn't going to put herself in that predicament ever again."

"Are you okay with that?"

"Sure. I don't ride—never did."

"But Noreen did."

"Yeah. It was through Barb that we met."

Kathy nodded, still not understanding why Noreen had decided to short-shrift her sister-in-law. Out of jealousy? Maybe. It wasn't something Kathy would have thought Noreen was capable of. She'd always seemed so *nice*. Kathy decided not to deliver the bad news to Paul, but she'd have some choice words for Noreen later on.

"I'd better get back to the bar. We open in just a few minutes."

"Yeah. And don't worry, I'll make sure your sister has a shower to remember."

"Thanks, Kath. You're the best."

Kathy nodded, walked Paul to the door, and saw him out. She tossed the damp towel over her shoulder, grabbed her phone, and stabbed the contacts icon, choosing Tori's number. Kathy didn't have time for a pre-call text. If Paul's sister was to have a happy party, it was up to Kathy to make it happen.

"Hello."

"Hello, Houston," Kathy said. "We have a problem."

∼

Tori closed her shop and arrived minutes after Kathy's call and simply said, "Put me to work."

Kathy had already hauled up the tote with the bridal booty and put Tori in charge of decorating the parlor. "Anissa should be here in a few minutes."

"You called her?"

"Yeah. Better think of something for her to do, too."

"Right."

Meanwhile, Kathy had checked her inventory in the big freezer in the butler's pantry. Muffins, muffins, muffins. Well, she figured, slap some frosting on them, and they're instant cupcakes. She also had some frozen appetizers she could pop in the oven once the guests had arrived. And she had an assortment of frozen cookies. If she started now, they'd be thawed by the time the guests showed up.

She was pulling out the ingredients for the frosting when Anissa arrived. "What's going on? I got a frantic call from Tori saying you had an emergency—but that I didn't need to bring my tools."

"Can you frost a cupcake?"

"One?" Anissa asked.

"More like twenty."

Anissa shrugged. "Maybe not bakery quality, but it can't be any harder than slapping joint compound on a wall, can it?"

"Nope."

They worked as a team. While Kathy prepared the frosting, Anissa arranged cookies on platters and three-tiered plate stands. Kathy set up her coffee maker for regular and decaf, then hauled out the cups and saucers. She had enough ingredients to make a sparking punch with a ginger ale base and figured she could plop in dollops of vanilla ice cream as a crowning touch. The appetizers were placed on trays, ready to pop into the oven.

It was almost two o'clock, and Kathy had just enough time to change into what she thought of as her hostess dress, when the bride arrived with her matron of honor, Ashley. After introducing them, Barb looked around the parlor. "Wow. Noreen was right. Your house is gorgeous. And the decorations are perfect."

Tori stood to one side and positively beamed.

"What do I need to do?" Barb asked.

Kathy turned and picked up a couple of objects. "First, you can put on this sash—and then, if you want, this tiara."

Barb's mouth dropped. "Oh, I'd look silly in a tiara. Wouldn't I?" she asked her friend.

"How often do you get to be a princess for a day?" Ashley said, amused.

Barb giggled. "Okay."

Kathy took their jackets, and the women sat down in the parlor to wait for the other guests.

"Do you need our help serving?" Tori asked.

"I've got it from here," Kathy assured her friends.

Anissa shook her head. "I wanna hear all the details on what went down this evening. I'll bring the wine."

"You got it, girlfriend," Kathy said. "And thank you guys so much. I couldn't have pulled this off without your help."

"What're friends for?" Tori asked.

Yeah. And did they still consider Noreen a friend?

The party was in full swing when Noreen arrived—twenty minutes late—dressed in her usual bar attire of a black T-shirt, black sweatpants, and black track shoes. She stood behind the big oak door and hadn't ventured into the parlor where the guests were playing a game of "Who knows the bride best." It was the look on Noreen's face that caused Kathy to pause before she moved forward to meet her next-door neighbor.

"Noreen, I expected you to be here long before this," Kathy said in greeting. Okay, it wasn't a happy greeting, but it was a greeting.

Noreen stepped forward enough to see the streamers and other decorations that adorned the room. "I told you that you didn't need to do anything—that I would take care of everything."

"Sorry, but when it became apparent you weren't going to get here in time for the shower, I had to take things into my own hands."

"We had a deal," Noreen said tersely. "I'm not paying for anything of this stuff." She sniffed the air. Kathy had put the first batch of mini quiches into the oven, and the heavenly aroma wafted through the home.

Kathy ignored Noreen's threat. "Hadn't you better go into the parlor and greet your guests?"

"They are not *my* guests."

"Someone invited them," Kathy said reasonably.

Another ripple of laughter cut the air.

Noreen straightened, her sullen expression transforming into a wan facsimile of a benign expression. She took a breath and charged past Kathy, entering the parlor.

"Girls, look! It's my sister-in-law, Noreen. Isn't she a doll for arranging all this?" Barb called.

Kathy tiptoed to the parlor's threshold to peek inside.

"It was nothing," Noreen demurred and seemed to be taking in all that Tori had done to decorate the space, along with the bowls of nuts, candy, and chips that Kathy had supplied. "It was nothing. Believe me, it was nothing," Noreen said with an odd inflection.

Barb was so happy she didn't seem to take in Noreen's increasingly angry countenance.

"We should get back to the game," Ashley said. "Noreen, would you like to play?"

"Oh, no. I'm so sorry, Barb, but I can't stay. We got a last-minute reservation for a funeral group. I have to get back to the grill. But I wanted to stop in and wish you well. Save me a slice of cake, will you?" she said with forced cheer.

Barb practically beamed. "You bet."

Noreen waved a cheerful good-bye to the group before heading for the door, with Kathy close on her heels.

Noreen clutched the handle and turned it, but Kathy's voice stopped her.

"Were you deliberately trying to humiliate Barb in front of her friends and family?" she accused.

Noreen turned, her eyes wide with innocence. "I don't know what you mean."

"Oh, yes, you do. You were intending that there only be a quarter sheet cake and nothing else for the ladies to eat, knowing they probably skipped lunch because they expected to be fed."

"I intended to do more. Knowing the bar was going to be hit with thirty people expecting to be fed after the funeral, I had a lot of prep to get done. I simply ran out of time."

Knowing she had a party to cater, Noreen could have told the funeral party The Bay Bar couldn't accommodate them, but Kathy had a feeling the whole excuse was a bald-faced lie. She was sure she could discover if it was true just by asking Eric the next time she saw him—and she fully intended to do so.

Noreen threw open the door and launched herself onto the porch. She didn't even bother to shut the door. She just trundled down the steps and headed toward the bar.

The oven timer went off, and Kathy closed the door and hurried toward the kitchen. She still had a bunch of hungry women to feed.

CHAPTER 15

The last of the guests were gathering their jackets, hugging the bride one last time, and leaving when Paul returned to Swans Nest. "Aw, damn. I was hoping to take pictures," he told Kathy.

"You can take a picture of the haul," she said with a laugh.

The presents were piled on one of the chairs, and the pretty greeting cards were lined up on the fireplace mantel.

"Yeah," he agreed and pulled out his phone. He took a few shots of the bride-to-be with her gifts and cards, and then they began to pack everything up to leave. On a trip back from the car, Paul turned to Kathy. "Where's Noreen?"

"She had to leave. Said something about a big funeral group to feed," Kathy said offhandedly.

Paul frowned. "Nothing's going on at the bar. In fact, we only turned three tables all afternoon."

Kathy shrugged, saying nothing.

Barb turned to Kathy. "Thank you for a terrific wedding shower. I'm going to tell all my friends about Swans Nest." Then she laughed. "Of course, most of them were already here, so they know what a beautiful home you have and what a great party you throw."

"I was happy to do it," Kathy said sincerely.

Barb lunged forward and hugged her. "Thanks again."

"I'll walk you to your car," Paul said and exited the inn.

Kathy bustled around the parlor, putting the furniture back in place. She'd vacuum later. As they'd used paper plates and plastic cutlery, she didn't have much to do in the kitchen except wash the cutlery, platters, teacups, and punch bowl. She filled the left side of the sink with hot, soapy water and put the cake-encrusted utensils in there to soak.

She heard the front door open and close, and soon Paul was standing in her kitchen. "Hey, Kath, I didn't see an entry in our checkbook to pay for this soiree. Did Noreen pay you in cash?"

"Uh, No. We agreed on a price, but I guess it slipped her mind," Kathy said casually.

"Well, let me know what we owe you, and I'll write you a check."

Kathy took a breath and swallowed before answering. "Fifty dollars."

Paul blinked. "That's impossible. I run a restaurant. I know what it costs to feed—let alone entertain—fifteen-plus people, and it ain't fifty bucks."

"That was the price Noreen negotiated," Kathy said, keeping her voice neutral.

Paul's eyes widened. "What were you supposed to provide for that?"

"The venue."

Paul raised an eyebrow. "But there were decorations. Barb said you put on a fantastic spread."

"I thought your sister deserved to have a lovely bridal shower. Wasn't that what she was expecting?"

Then it seemed to dawn on Paul just what Kathy was saying.

"Yes, she did deserve to have a nice afternoon with her friends and family." His gaze traveled to the floor. "If you give me an itemized bill, I'll write you a check."

"You don't have to do that," Kathy said. "I just used what I had on hand and leftover decorations from the other bridal showers I hosted."

"Well, everything looked perfect. You put in a lot of effort for a stranger."

"You're not a stranger, and so by association, neither is your sister."

Paul's voice broke when he spoke again. "Thank you."

"It was my pleasure."

"Uh, I need to get back to the bar. The dinner crowd is probably already starting to assemble."

"It's that time of day," Kathy agreed.

Paul nodded and turned for the door. But he paused before turning the handle. "Thanks for what you did for my sister. I'll never forget it."

"Like I said, it was my pleasure."

It was with rounded shoulders that Paul left Swans Nest.

Kathy was grateful she hadn't had to tattle on Noreen, letting Paul come to his own conclusions. It was obvious what Noreen had tried to pull on her sister-in-law, and Kathy had a feeling there'd be hell to pay for it.

While she didn't smile, she didn't feel bad for Noreen, either. She wondered how Paul would handle the discussion ... and wished she could be a fly on the wall when it happened.

~

Tori and Anissa were waiting in the bungalow's kitchen, wine glasses in front of them and ready to pour when Kathy walked through the door just after five.

"Well?" Anissa demanded.

"I think I lost my serving job," Kathy said, shrugging out of her jacket and hanging it on a peg by the door.

Tori winced. "I take it Noreen found out about the elves who helped the shoemaker," she said, calling back on something Anissa had said days before.

"I don't look like no elf," Anissa said in her best urban cadence.

"I bet you'd look cute sitting on a shelf," Tori teased.

"Green is not my color," Anissa said flatly.

Kathy retrieved the wine from the fridge, sat at her usual place at the table, and poured it.

"Spill all," Tori demanded.

She did.

"Talk about petty," Tori muttered after Kathy's recitation.

"What was that woman thinking trying to screw her husband's sister? She had to know that wouldn't go down well," Anissa remarked.

"And now I betrayed her by giving Barb the shower she deserved," Kathy said sadly.

"She enjoyed herself?" Tori asked.

"Barb was over the moon when she left. *I* was over the moon when most of the ladies took brochures for Swans Nest home with them."

"Nothing like some good word of mouth to get the PR wagon rolling," Anissa said and drained her glass.

"So what are you going to do come Monday, and you're supposed to show up at the bar for your shift?" Tori asked.

"I'm not going. Didn't Herb say there was an opening at Tom's Grocery in Warton? I may as well head out that way tomorrow, and put in an application."

"I need to buy some things for tomorrow's dinner anyway, like the main course. I was going to go today, but after I left Swans Nest, I just didn't feel like it. I figured I'd go to the store right after it opens tomorrow and that'll give me plenty of time to pull off a dinner for my Gramps." She glanced in Anissa's direction. "You're welcome to come. It might only be chicken, but I'm going to try to pull off a mini-Thanksgiving dinner because Gramps might not come back north until next summer."

"I'd be happy to join you," Anissa said. "What can I bring?"

"Dessert?"

Anissa frowned. "That's Kathy's forte, not mine. But I make a mean sweet potato casserole."

"Then you can bring that. Thanks."

"I'll do dessert," Kathy offered. "Something decadent. Any requests?"

Tori thought about it for a moment. "Gramps loves lemon meringue pie."

"Not exactly decadent, but I can pull it off."

"Great," Tori said.

The camaraderie around the table took a downward turn when Anissa voiced what was on her mind. "Does this whole thing with Noreen mean we can't go to The Bay Bar anymore?"

"We might have to get our fish-fry fixes at some dive at Lotus Point," Tori lamented.

"It's gonna be a slippery drive come winter," Anissa commented. She frowned.

"You guys don't have to avoid the bar just because Noreen is angry with me," Kathy said.

"Yeah, like she's going to make it comfortable for us to be there," Anissa pointed out.

"Well, she does stay in the kitchen most of the time. Usually, when we go there, Paul gives her a shout, and *then* she comes out for a visit."

Anissa nodded. "I kinda liked Noreen before learning about this awful aspect of her personality."

"Yeah, why would anyone be so threatened by their husband's relationship with a sibling?" Tori wondered.

Kathy shrugged. "Who knows."

"Was there anything weird about Paul's sister?" Anissa asked.

"Not that I could tell. But the fact that Noreen put zero effort into the party she volunteered to host says a lot. I think she wanted to humiliate Barb in front of her friends. I can't imagine why anyone would do that."

"Me, either," Anissa quipped.

"I never figured Noreen to be the insecure type. What kind of trauma causes someone to act that way?" Tori wondered.

"Who says she suffered trauma? Maybe she's just a 'Karen' who has to have everything her own way," Anissa suggested.

"Karens have a bad reputation. You always see them at their worst. I always wonder what powder keg they've been straddling and for how long before some stupid, and usually insignificant thing, sets them off."

"You are *too* nice a person—always seeing the good in people," Anissa accused.

"That's because I *want* to believe that most people are inherently good and that they just have really bad, no good, terrible days."

"And then have to live the rest of their lives under a rock in shame," Tori added.

"Yeah," Kathy agreed sadly. "At least Noreen wasn't caught on video being despicable—and I'm sure Paul isn't going to admit to Barb that Noreen was acting like a total piece of crap. But still—*he* knows. That's got to be a real strain on their relationship going forward."

"Yeah," Tori agreed sadly.

Kathy poured another round of wine. "Did you hear from Detective Osborn about Mrs. Stanton's situation?"

Tori shook her head. "I really didn't think I would."

"I been thinking about the dead guy a lot," Anissa said and shuddered, probably remembering his charred hands and the frozen look of shock on his face. "It just doesn't seem like murder to me."

"Why do you say that?" Kathy asked.

"For one, there are easier ways to kill a guy. Guns, knives, poisoned pizza."

"Poisoned pizza?" Tori asked.

"Sure, you could disguise it in pickled peppers or something."

"Who has pickled peppers on their pizza?" Kathy asked.

Anissa lifted her glass. "Probably the same ones who eat it with pineapple." She gave another little shudder.

"But a crime *was* committed," Tori pointed out.

"What crime?" Kathy asked.

"Moving the body to Anissa's boat."

Anissa laughed. "Maybe Noreen did it."

"Ha-ha," Tori deadpanned.

"You'd have to be awfully strong to do that," Kathy pointed out, ignoring Anissa's not-so-funny joke. "Stanton wasn't a featherweight."

"Coulda been a couple of people. We don't know who or how many guys Stanton owed money to," Tori remarked.

The others nodded.

"The sad thing is that we may never find out what happened to that man."

"Or probably his widow. Seems like she's the real victim here," Kathy said.

Tori and Anissa nodded. There didn't seem to be anything else to add, at least on that subject.

"Let's talk about food," Tori suggested. "So far, we've got chicken, sweet potato casserole, stuffing, and pie."

"You need a green vegetable," Kathy said. 'Green bean casserole."

"Ugh! No!" Anissa asserted.

"I agree," Tori said. "Broccoli? Brussels sprouts? Salad? Squash?"

"Squash is too close to sweet potatoes," Anissa said. "Besides, it's not green."

"What did your grandmother make for Thanksgiving?" Kathy asked.

"Boiled Brussels sprouts. I'm not sure anybody but her ever ate them."

"Have you ever roasted them? They're really good roasted. And what about the versatile potato? You can boil, mash, roast, or fry them."

"Mashed—with homemade gravy," Anissa agreed. "And ya gotta have lumps in the potatoes so the guests know they aren't reconstituted."

"Who makes instant mashed potatoes?" Tori asked.

"My mother," Anissa said. "She hates to cook. She'll take any shortcut to put a meal on the table. She sees food as sustenance—not as an enjoyable experience."

"How sad," Kathy remarked.

"What are we going to drink?" Anissa asked.

"Gramps prefers beer."

"We prefer wine," Kathy said.

"Why can't we have both?" Anissa asked.

Tori shook her head. "Why not? Or I could get some sparkling grape juice."

"It's not much cheaper than wine," Anissa pointed out. "I'll bring a nice white—it goes good with chicken."

"Problem solved," Kathy said, leaning back in her chair.

Tori nodded, her gaze falling to the table.

"What's wrong, Tor?" Kathy asked.

Tori shrugged. "There was so much going on at the auction Friday night, Gramps didn't have time to—" She paused. Did he want to interrogate or berate her? Neither, it turned out, but both were a distinct possibility.

Anissa seemed to have gained psychic powers by saying, "Think positive. If your grandpaw is crabby at you, you only have to take it for a few hours. He'll be gone Monday, and then only be a grinch once a week on your Sunday calls."

"I don't like to think of him like that," Tori protested, but inwardly she had to admit that Anissa had a point—and probably because her relationship with her mother mirrored what Tori and Herb experienced.

"We are going to have a lovely dinner tomorrow afternoon. Do I make myself clear?" Kathy announced.

Anissa grimaced before saluting. "Yes, ma'am."

Kathy glared at Tori.

"If you say so."

"I do." But Tori's eye was still a shade of purple. She might be able to cover most of it with makeup, but she still had to wait to see if the school would invite her back. Maybe she'd visit the high school on Monday and visit the nurse to see if she thought Tori was ready to return to the classroom. The thing was, the whole school knew that Bradley Hughes had clocked her. Surely some of them would be on her side…or didn't that matter to the district?

She hadn't had a customer in days. Most of the boats in her marina were gone for the season. Don Newton got most of the business this time of year simply because he had a bigger parking lot and a wider supply of snacks.

I won't think about it, Tori told herself and forced a smile.

"Kathy's right. We're going to have a lovely dinner—and I'm going to win Gramps over."

"I can wear him down with a detailed walk through the Lotus Lodge," Anissa volunteered. "Believe me, I know more about plumbing, drywall, and conduit than most women on the planet."

"And I can bore him in detail on how to put on one helluva good wedding shower," Kathy volunteered.

Tori laughed. "You guys are the best."

"I ain't no guy. I'm a woman," Anissa asserted.

"Me, too," Kathy agreed, hoisting her glass with the tiniest of sips left in it.

"I think we need another round," Anissa said. "Besides, these are awfully small glasses."

"They are," Kathy agreed and uncapped the wine once more to pour.

"You guys are crazy."

Anissa gave Tori the eye.

"Okay, you *gals* are crazy."

"That's better," Anissa said, holding out her glass for Kathy to fill. Next, she filled Tori's glass. "Tor, never fear—you've got two friends here who will always have your back—just like we know you'll always have ours."

"Like the Three Musketeers?"

"The female version," Anissa asserted.

"All for one and one for all!" Kathy crowed.

They clinked glasses.

CHAPTER 16

*T*om's Grocery opened at 8 am, and Tori and Kathy were on the road just after that to get what they'd need for the upcoming feast.

Tori chose a small cart. Thanks to Anissa filling the fridge days before, she really only needed to buy a chicken, a loaf of bread, and some celery for the stuffing. Kathy needed eggs and a fresh lemon.

They had only just put the bread into the cart when they heard a familiar voice.

"Damn, I should've called you, and we could've ridden in together," Anissa called as she approached with a blue-plastic shopping basket draped over her arm. "Then again, you probably wouldn't have wanted to go with me to give an estimate for repairing a roof up on Furnace Road."

"Probably not," Kathy agreed.

"I was going to call you gals," Anissa said, lowering her voice, "about something I saw on the way down Resort Road."

"What's that?"

"Well, you know Lucinda Bloomfield's land butts up to the last house on the street."

"So?"

"I noticed some of the high-tension lines are hanging low."

Tori blinked. "Do you think Chuck Stanton was killed on her property?"

"We know from experience how loyal her employees are—and that she pays them well enough that they'd likely try to protect her from scandal."

Tori frowned. "I can't imagine they wouldn't report an accidental death that happened on her property."

"But what if it *wasn't* an accident?" Anissa insisted. Lucinda and her staff hadn't exactly harassed Anissa's father, but they had made his life difficult, pestering him to sell what looked like his decaying home. Little did anyone know that while the outside of the home looked decrepit, the inside was filled with beautifully handcrafted furniture and high-end finishes. He just liked to bug Lucinda. His daughter felt the same when she came to live at the home.

Kathy frowned. "Why didn't Detective Osborn and the guys from the power company see or check those wires when they were at your place?"

Anissa chewed her bottom lip, looking just a little guilty before she spoke again. "Well, they would have had to trespass on her property to do so."

"And what were *you* doing trespassing on her property?" Tori asked.

"I wasn't exactly trespassing. It's just that—"

"What?" Tori insisted.

Anissa looked embarrassed. "Okay, I *wasn't* driving past her property. There's an old orchard. It's not *on* her property but behind the old Hanson place."

"And?" Kathy prompted.

"I kind of picked a few apples."

"Old orchard," Kathy repeated. "Are the apples full of worms because they're not sprayed?"

"They're not *full* of worms. You just have to be careful when eating them. In fact, I *don't* just eat them. Last fall, I made six jars of applesauce. I'm meticulous to make sure the parts I eat don't have pests. I like to think of them as organic and pesticide-free."

"They sure are," Tori agreed.

"Yeah, and I've made apple pies with them, too. Pretty tasty."

Anissa had brought one of her apple pies down to the compound. It *was* pretty good, too.

"Anyway, I was wondering if I should call Detective Osborn and tell him about the low-hanging wires."

Another customer wandered up, chose a package of hot dog buns, and meandered off. They waited until she was well out of earshot before continuing their conversation.

"Maybe calling Osborn wouldn't be a good idea," Tori said. "I mean if he's hot to pin this accident on you."

"Yeah," Kathy agreed.

"So are you two going to snoop around instead and maybe call him yourself?" Anissa asked.

"Gee, I dunno," Tori said. "What excuse could we use to tell him about the wires?"

"Yeah," Kathy agreed.

"You were just taking a walk and—"

"Leaving the road and walking on someone's private property?" Kathy exclaimed, and rather loudly. One of the cashiers turned to look at the women. They turned their backs on the cashier.

"I dunno...I'd have to think about it," Tori said.

"Well, don't think too long," Anissa said. "Else, I could be sitting in a jail cell at the county seat."

"Don't talk like that," Kathy chided her.

"I have to think about my future, and I don't want to spend it in a cell at the women's prison in Albion."

"Okay," Tori said, hoping to placate their friend. "We'll think of some excuse to go up there and look."

Anissa retrieved her phone, tapped on the screen, and took in the time. "I need to get out of here and go give that estimate. I'll swing by the liquor store on my way back. It'll be open by then."

"Sounds like a plan," Kathy said.

"We'll see you this afternoon. Gramps is supposed to come around three, but we aren't eating until at least four, so come when you want to."

"Will do," Anissa said, "But first, I need to find me a couple of big, sweet potatoes and get some marshmallows."

While Anissa picked out a couple of yams, Kathy sorted through the lemons until she found a couple that pleased her. Tori wasn't nearly as picky when it came to choosing celery. They said good-bye and headed for the meat department, where Tori opted for an eight-pound chicken. If they didn't eat the whole thing, she could at least get a lunch or two of chicken salad sandwiches out of the bird.

They were about to head for the check-out counters when Tori caught sight of a familiar figure and gasped. "Oh no!" she whispered hoarsely. "It's Bradley Hughes!"

"Where?" Kathy asked, looking around.

Tori steered her cart away from the meat counter and ducked into the cat and dog food aisle. Hopefully, Bradley hadn't seen her. She hadn't realized how upset she'd feel upon seeing the young man again. What was he doing at the grocery store so early on a Sunday morning? She thought most teens would be in bed until noon—if their parents let them sleep in.

She watched as Bradley strode to the back of the store, where the beer was kept in a big cold locker. Thinking fast, Tori whipped out her phone and started filming as Bradley pulled out a 12-pack of Genessee cream ale, what people in these parts called beer on training wheels. As Bradley approached, she shoved her phone into Kathy's hands and whispered, "Take over."

Kathy dutifully took the phone but turned away from Bradley's advancing figure to not draw attention to herself. Once he passed, Kathy charged down the aisle, pausing at the end and aiming the phone's camera in the direction of check-out lane 2. Tori was close behind her, taking in the spectacle. Bradley presented an ID and the young girl scrutinized it before she rang up the sale.

Oh, boy. Not only could Bradly get into serious trouble but so could the store if something happened. Like a DUI. Either way, Tori had evidence against the bully who'd flattened her almost a week before.

Now, all she had to do was figure out how to use it to her advantage.

~

Tori and Kathy decided to a ride by the property near Anissa's home, which she'd described as having the hanging power lines. They parked in Anissa's driveway.

"We can't be too long," Kathy advised. "That chicken needs to be kept cold."

"We'll be fifteen minutes at the most," Tori said as they set off across the street. The Old Hanson place wasn't as old and derelict as the moniker might have hinted. It was the only other summer cottage on the road, but unlike its nearest neighbor—Eric Mooney's house—The Hanson place was neat, tidy, and looked like it had been painted just that summer. It also looked to be closed for the winter, although that date on the calendar was two months away.

The women looked around—and saw no one in sight—before traipsing across the lawn bordering Lucinda Bloomfield's estate.

"What exactly are we looking for."

"Duh—sagging wires."

"I didn't mean that. I mean, what good is it going to do to pinpoint where that poor man died?"

Tori shrugged and kept walking, glad she'd worn long pants,

socks, and work boots. The grass wasn't as short the farther they went, and didn't tick season last until at least the first frost? Kathy wore slacks, socks, and sneakers. She'd probably be okay.

They came upon the remnants of the old orchard Anissa had mentioned. Some of the apples had already fallen. Tori plucked one from the tree and examined it. Yup—wormholes, but not many. She would see it might be worth cutting out that part and not wasting the rest. And she doubted anyone would care if Anissa pinched a few apples for herself.

Finally, they came up to a line of thick wooden poles sporting thick black cables. As Anissa had said, there was a sag in the thickest cable near a huge gray cylinder—a transformer—and was that blackened flesh still adhering to the plastic coating? It made her shiver to think about it. Still, she forced herself to study the scene. Something wasn't right, but she couldn't put her finger on it. Taking out her phone, she snapped a few photos. Like the video of underage Bradley buying beer, she didn't know what she would do with them, but she felt it was worth it to chronicle what she saw.

"Why are there large power lines in the back of the properties when there are also poles with wires on the street side?" Kathy asked.

"That's a good question. Maybe they service the houses east of Resort Road."

There weren't many houses in that area, but area farms alternated planting fields of corn and soybeans from year to year.

Tori studied the parallel rows of cables that stretched from Ridge Road in the south to north through the Bloomfield estate and beyond. Except for the dip in the cable, there was nothing much to see.

Tori took another look around and pivoted. "We'd better get home and put that poor chicken in the fridge before it develops a temperature."

"Finally," Kathy muttered. "I've got a pie to make—and I want that meringue to be sky high."

"I'm sure my Gramps will appreciate it," Tori said.

Tori was preoccupied as they walked back to the truck. It wasn't what she saw; it was what she *hadn't* seen: no sign of a ladder. The guy hadn't been wearing cleats or other safety equipment for climbing poles when Tori and Anissa found him. The grass hadn't been trampled and had probably grown a bit since the "accident." Did that mean Stanton hadn't been dragged? That said, it was quite a trek to the road—a long way to carry a dead weight. It didn't make sense.

The women climbed into the truck. Tori backed out of Anissa's driveway and slowly started up Resort Road.

"Wow, Eric's yard looks almost tidy," Kathy remarked as they passed.

Tori took in the scene. "Yeah. Now, if he could just spruce up the house, Lucinda might become his friend, too."

Kathy stifled a laugh. "As if."

"Stranger things have happened."

Yeah, and whoever moved Stanton's body had probably been strange, too.

CHAPTER 17

Herb Cannon was late and didn't arrive until just before four o'clock that Sunday afternoon, parking his rental car in front of the bungalow and entering his former home without a knock.

Tori stood in front of the stove, testing the potatoes to see if they were cooked through. "Hey, Gramps," she called, "glad you could make it. Can I get you a beer?"

Herb took off his jacket, sliding it onto the farthest peg on the wall—where it had probably resided in years past. "I can get it myself," he said, striding to the fridge, yanking it open, and taking out a bottle of Sam Adams, what Tori remembered he'd drunk in the past. He didn't bother with a glass but moved to one of the cutlery drawers and yanked it open. "Hey, where's my bottle opener? It sat in that drawer for at least forty years."

Kathy appeared on the scene. "Sorry, Mr. Cannon, but I've rearranged the kitchen to suit my needs."

"Yeah, Kathy's the one who does most of the cooking around here. I'm just playing make-believe chef today," Tori explained.

Kathy directed Herb to one of the other drawers, where he

found the church key and flipped the lid on his beer. He took a swig and grinned. "Mighty fine."

A knock sounded on the door, which opened, allowing Anissa to enter carrying a vintage Pyrex dish swaddled by worn potholders. "Hope I'm not too late," she called. She set the casserole on the counter and removed her coat, placing it on the hook next to Herb's. "How soon are we going to eat?"

"Probably not for another ten or twenty minutes," Tori said.

"Can I put the casserole in your oven?"

"Of course," Kathy said. Anissa carried the casserole over to the stove while Kathy opened the oven. Inside it went. "Want some wine?"

"Does a bear—" Anissa hesitated, "poop in the woods?"

"I thought you might say that," Kathy said. Three wine glasses lined the counter, and she passed one to Anissa before heading to the fridge to get a bottle."

"Shoot, I've got a new one in my truck. Let me go get it and we can stick it in the fridge to keep it cool."

And with that, Anissa dashed out the door.

"You girls drink too much," Herb said and took another swig of his beer.

Tori gave Kathy a meaningful look but said nothing.

Anissa soon returned with the bottle, stashing it in the fridge, and Kathy poured from the opened bottle.

"Sit down, you guys," Tori encouraged from her position at the stove.

"Can I help with anything?" Kathy asked.

"Nope." The truth was, Kathy made the stuffing, cut up the vegetables, and opened the can of cranberry sauce. Tori had just tossed the chicken in the oven and boiled the veggies, although she might let Kathy mash the potatoes—and hopefully to Anissa's preferred level of lumpiness.

"Something sure smells good," Herb commented, taking his

old seat at the table. Tori would have to plop elsewhere. That was okay. It was only for one night.

"So, what's going on with you girls?"

Tori turned to see Anissa wince. She did *not* like being called a girl.

"I got a call from one of the ladies who came to the bridal shower I threw yesterday at Swans Nest," Kathy said.

"And—and?" Tori asked, captivated.

"She wants to book a romantic weekend with her husband before the holidays."

"That's great," Tori said, not hiding her enthusiasm.

"Even better, she's trying to convince her best friend to book for the same weekend."

"Let's hope your freebie wedding shower pays off big time," Anissa said, raising her glass in salute.

Herb frowned. "What free wedding shower?" Was he going to be upset that Kathy hadn't offered him a free ride during his next visit but had done so for a complete stranger? Suddenly, Tori wished Kathy hadn't said a word.

"Maybe that'll make up for losing your job at The Bay Bar," Anissa said. A look in Herb's direction—and his scowl—caused Anissa to grimace.

"You lost your job, too?" he accused.

"Not that she knows—yet," Tori amended.

"It's a long, drawn-out story that you don't want to hear, Mr. Cannon." Kathy began.

"And why wouldn't I?" he asked, his voice hardening.

"Mostly because we don't have confirmation, but—"

"I'd like to know, if you don't mind."

Tori would bet Kathy *did* mind, but she also knew Kathy had become adept at placating the compound's former owner.

Kathy explained how Noreen hadn't finalized any plans for the wedding shower, only to supply a tiny cake that would not feed the fifteen guests who'd arrived.

Tori was proud of how Kathy related the story with a neutral tone.

"That doesn't sound good," Herb grudgingly agreed.

"How long have you known Paul, Mr. Cannon," Anissa asked.

Herb shrugged. "Ever since he bought the bar."

"And Noreen?"

"Not so much," he admitted.

"I just don't understand how one woman could do that to another woman?" Kathy said.

Anissa laughed. "Girl, did you just get off the banana boat? Women have been trained from the get-go—and not necessarily by men—to be catty to each other."

"Well, that hasn't been my experience."

"It's sure been mine," Tori muttered.

"And mine, too," Anissa said, and the women clinked glasses.

"Well, I don't want to believe it happens all the time."

"Girl, you saw it in real time just yesterday," Anissa pushed.

"Well, I hope Noreen has a good reason for acting that way."

"Let me know when humiliation becomes the law of the land so I can disaffect," Anissa muttered and sipped her wine.

An awkward silence followed.

"What do you hear about the dead guy?" Herb asked, changing the subject.

"I think Stanton's death was an accident," Tori said and got up to check on the potatoes again.

"I agree," Anissa confirmed.

"We checked out the power lines you told us about," Kathy said, and Tori explained to Herb their foray earlier in the day.

"But there's still the problem of hauling Stanton's bulk across the compound's parking lot, down the dock, and dumping it into Anissa's aluminum boat."

"Just because I'm a woman with curves—and biceps," Anissa said, "Detective Osborn seems to think I might have been able to do that deed."

"More like your height," Herb said. "You *are* a statuesque woman."

Anissa looked thoughtful. "I never thought of myself that way, but I guess when you're five ten people might think of you as that."

Herb nodded. "Your theory sounds about right. I did hear that someone from the power company could be persuaded to do illegal hookups—for a price."

"That doesn't make sense," Tori said. "If someone couldn't pay their utility bills, how could they afford to pay off Stanton?"

Herb looked thoughtful. "Well, say the guy—and I never heard it was Stanton—first charged a modest price to do the hookup and then blackmailed the person—or persons—to pay him more and more every month or threaten to turn them in."

"Yeah, but couldn't they just turn around and accuse Stanton of doing the hookup and blackmail?"

"Think about it," Herb said rationally. "The people this blackmailer would be harassing wouldn't have to pay a lot a month—just enough to keep them under his thumb."

"And that would be enough to keep him going to Batavia Downs for the slots and other games," Kathy said.

"More likely he dealt with a bookie if what his wife has intimated is true," Herb said.

Tori frowned. "Where would someone find a bookie here in Ward County?"

Herb looked over the lenses of his glasses to glare at his granddaughter. "You don't want to know."

Tori thought about what she'd seen that morning. Now wasn't the time to review her phone photos, but she'd do so after Herb left.

The potatoes were done. Tori grabbed the meat thermometer from one of the drawers, removed the chicken from the oven, and stabbed it with the probe. The numbers ticked up until it hit

173 degrees. Taking the box of aluminum foil from another drawer, Tori wrapped the bird and set it aside to rest.

"You wanna mash those potatoes, Kath?" Tori asked.

"Can do," Kathy said and leapt into action.

"Everything sure smells good," Herb said, which, coming from him, was high praise.

Tori's heart swelled with affection. "Would you like to carve the bird?"

Herb looked thoughtful. "I haven't been asked to do that since the last time your grandma cooked a Thanksgiving dinner."

"Well, we'll just have to put you to work more often," Tori said.

While Herb did an excellent job with the chicken, Tori assembled the side dishes, Kathy poured the drinks, and Anissa finished setting the table. They sat down to eat, and Tori gave silent thanks to be with her Gramps and two best friends.

It truly felt like Thanksgiving.

CHAPTER 18

Herb didn't leave until almost eight—obviously in no hurry to catch up on news of the baby shower. For the rest of the evening, Tori wrestled with her conscience, trying to decide what to do with the video of an underage Bradley buying beer. Would it look like an act of revenge after he'd assaulted her or a private citizen reporting a crime—a crime that could potentially have lethal consequences? Maybe not on that day, but if the behavior was repeated.... Tori didn't like to think about it.

When she'd taught English in her old district, one of her students bought beer, drank too much, and crashed his car. It was the talk of the school when the boy was about to be taken off life support. His father had forced his son's friends to look at his brain-dead and swollen, bruised body in a hospital bed, tied to life support machines, and let them know that he was about to be disconnected and his organs donated. The students had been shattered. It was a brutal life lesson, and Tori was grateful the dad had had the intestinal fortitude to impress upon his popular son's peers the consequences of disobeying the law and how life-changing—and ending—such decisions could be.

And so, Tori got up early the next morning, making herself a cup of tea before sitting down at her computer and writing an email to Detective Osborn, explaining the situation and attaching the video she and Kathy had made the previous day. Bradley hadn't seen her or Kathy. Hopefully he will never find out who gave the video to law enforcement. And if nothing ever came of it, then so be it. Tori had done her civic duty.

With that task done, Tori decided to leave her home office. She didn't have the stomach to check frivolous social media posts. She ended up in the kitchen, poured and reheated another cup of tea, and was still sitting in quiet contemplation when Kathy appeared an hour later, tousle-haired and yawning, dressed in her bathrobe and fuzzy slippers.

"Did you have breakfast?" Kathy asked and measured the water to put in the coffeemaker.

Tori shook her head. She didn't want to mention her email. "No, I've just been sitting here for a while thinking about things."

"Things?"

"And people. And the stupid mistakes they make."

"Do you want to share any of that with me?"

Tori shrugged. "Mostly Bradley Hughes."

Kathy nodded. "Yeah. Have you decided what to do with the video?"

"I sent it to Detective Osborn."

Kathy winced. "I'll bet Bradley is going to have a crappy day."

"As a teacher, I'm a mandated reporter. I'm required by law to report such things. It really wasn't a choice."

Kathy nodded, but she didn't quite look convinced. She took out a coffee filter and measured the grounds.

"Do you think I'm wrong?" Tori asked.

"No. I just worry what might happen if he finds out who turned him in."

"Yeah, but it was the right thing to do. It's too bad that doing the right thing can often feel scary."

"Yeah," Kathy agreed. "Hey, why don't we have a thoroughly fattening breakfast to cheer us up?"

"Tempt me," Tori deadpanned.

"French toast and bacon?"

Tori's eyebrows rose. "Sounds delish."

∼

HERB SHOWED up at the compound a little after nine on that morning. "I come to have a cup of coffee and to say good-bye for a while."

"Well, I hope you'll come back soon, Gramps. I don't feel like we got nearly enough time together," Tori said.

"Yeah, there's lots going on with Irene's family. Can't say it will be much different the next time we come—and she's got her heart set on Christmas—or thereabouts."

It had been years since Tori spent the holiday with her grandfather. She had no idea what to give a man who had the money to buy anything and everything, but she'd sure try.

Kathy appeared from the direction of the office. "Hey, Mr. Cannon. Did you come for breakfast?"

"No, just coffee," Herb said.

Kathy grabbed a clean cup for herself. "Oh, great—thanks for making a fresh pot, Tor."

"My pleasure."

"Are you sure you couldn't force yourself to have one of my lemon poppy seed scones? They're mighty tasty," Kathy teased.

Herb seemed to think it over. "Well, maybe just a small one. We aren't going to get lunch on the plane."

Kathy smiled. "Tor?"

"I'll have one, too," Tori said.

Kathy retrieved three of the scones from the freezer, set them on a plate, and nuked them for a minute. When the microwave beeped, Kathy poured herself a mug of coffee before she brought the plate to the table. She grabbed napkins from the holder and passed them around. "Dig in," she ordered.

Tori already knew how good the scones were, but Herb's eyes widened with pleasure on the first bite. "Good lord, these are tasty," he told Kathy. "If only Irene baked, I'd ask for the recipe."

"Why don't I bake a batch and mail them to you?"

"I sure wouldn't say no," Herb said, taking a larger bite, chewing, and closing his eyes, a smile brightening his face.

A knock at the door caused the three to look in that direction. Tori saw a man in a suit standing in front of the glass window. "What the heck?" she muttered and got up to answer the door.

"Ms. Victoria Cannon?"

"Yes," Tori said warily. Was she about to be served with a summons?

"My name is James Jenkins, Esquire, from the law firm of Bingham, Lewis, and Vandewater. May I have a word with you?"

Tori backed away from the door to let the attorney in and closed the door behind him. "Won't you sit down? Can I get you a cup of coffee?"

Jenkins took the remaining seat—the one that wasn't sporting scone crumbs. "No, thank you."

As Tori resumed her seat, Jenkins set his briefcase on the floor beside him. He fixed his gaze on Tori's still bruised face but didn't comment.

"What's this all about?" Herb asked.

"Oh, sorry. This is my grandfather, Herbert Cannon, and my roommate Kathy Grant."

Jenkins nodded. "Mr. Cannon." He didn't seem pleased to make Herb's acquaintance and totally ignored Kathy, turning his attention back to Tori.

"I'm sure you can guess why I'm here, Ms. Cannon."

"No, why don't you tell us," Tori said, although she had a pretty good idea why a lawyer might show up on her doorstep.

Jenkins cleared his throat. "I'm here on behalf of the parents of Bradley Hughes."

"The brute who clocked poor Tori," Herb stated with an edge to his tone.

"Er, yes." Jenkins turned his gaze toward Tori. "His parents, Beverly and Martin Hughes, have reached out to our firm to see if we can't rectify Bradley's unfortunate lack of judgment in his encounter with you last week at Warton High School."

"When he punched Tori out," Herb reiterated.

"We prefer to think of it as a misunderstanding," Jenkins persisted.

"Like hell," Herb muttered. "Let's cut to the chase. How much are you going to offer Tori not to sue the pants off the Hughes?"

Jenkins seemed to be sweating around the collar of his silk dress shirt. "That's what I'm here to discuss."

"Well, let me take a wild guess. If I'm not mistaken, young Bradley has been scouted by Penn State, or some other Big East college, and should he face a trial in a battery case, might lose whatever opportunity he has to be a gridiron star," Herb began.

Jenkins's discomfort seemed to increase. Was he the best a big-name firm like Bingham, Lewis, and Vandewater had to send out on a mission to buy off a possible litigant, or had they decided such a dumb rube school teacher from the sticks would lap up any figure they offered?

"Why don't we review what happened," Herb suggested. He nodded in Tori's direction, and gave her the go-ahead to tell her side of the story.

Jenkins listened but seemed bored by Tori's recitation. "Bradley has a different view of things. That said, we are prepared to make a substantial offer to settle the matter."

"And what do you consider substantial?" Kathy asked.

Jenkins took a breath before answering. "Two thousand dollars."

Silence greeted his statement.

"You're joking, right?" Herb asked.

"No, Mr. Cannon. I'm not."

"Hmm...now let me see if I remember what the penalty is for assault and battery. Jail time—from five to twenty-five years; fines up to a thousand dollars, and long-term probation—or all three."

Jenkins glowered. He turned his attention to Tori. "What figure were you thinking, Ms. Cannon?"

Tori probably would have settled for two grand if her grandfather hadn't spoken up.

"Not only did my granddaughter suffer from the physical assault, but she also lost the respect of her students. What price can someone put on that kind of degradation?" Herb demanded.

Jenkins seemed to squirm within his tailored suit. "I'm prepared to go as high as five thousand."

"Tori had to go to Urgent Care to get checked out. She isn't covered for that kind of expense," Herb added.

"We would, of course, reimburse her for that charge."

"Uh-huh," Herb said, sipping his coffee and grimacing. "Kathy, would you please give my cup a zap in the microwave?"

Kathy jumped up and accepted the offered mug. "Sure thing, Mr. Cannon."

They waited as the seconds ticked by until the microwave went *beep, beep, beep!* and Kathy presented Herb with his warm-up.

"Now, where were we?" Herb mused.

"Five thousand dollars plus expenses," Jenkins reiterated.

Herb shook his head. "It would be an awful shame if that young man's future were to be compromised. No scholarships. No NFL career."

"We're prepared to go to seven thousand," Jenkins offered.

Herb looked toward the ceiling. "Imagine a young man scarred by a battery conviction. It could affect every aspect of his future, from academics to job prospects. That kind of information on the Internet is forever. All someone would have to do is type that young man's name into a search box, and—BAM—that battery charge will follow him all the days of his life."

"Eight thousand dollars," Jenkins countered.

"How many students were in that classroom, Tori?" Herb asked.

"Uh, I believe twenty."

"Twenty witness to the assault," Herb said, shaking his head.

"Ten thousand," Jenkins said through gritted teeth.

Tori and Kathy exchanged looks. Ten grand could solve a lot of Tori's problems.

But then, Herb hitched up his hip and removed his cell phone from the clip on his belt. "And then there's the video evidence."

A tight-lipped Jenkins watched as Herb played a recording of what transpired a week before when Bradley Hughes assaulted Tori. He shoved the little screen in Jenkin's face and played it three times.

"I wonder what a sympathetic jury would say after seeing the evidence of this crime?" Herb posed.

Long seconds passed before Jenkins grimly said, "Twenty thousand, and that's my final offer."

Herb shook his head, turning to his granddaughter. "I don't know, Tori. What do you think?"

Tori's mouth had gone dry. From a low-ball offer of two grand to ten times as much in only a matter of minutes.... It was all she could do not to jump up from her seat and do a happy dance. Instead, she ducked her head, looking somber. "Well, I would hate to see Bradley's future ruined because of a youthful indiscretion." She paused, letting the silence lengthen. "I suppose I could accept that offer—with expenses," she amended.

"Of course," Jenkins said, looking positively dour. And with that, he picked up his briefcase, set it on the table, and withdrew a sheaf of papers. He'd been pretty smug, thinking that Tori would settle. That said, the only blank in the paperwork was the amount of the agreement.

"We'd like to read through those papers before Tori signs anything," Herb said.

"Of course," Jenkins agreed.

So, Tori, Herb, and Kathy meticulously went over the contract, and even left the room to discuss any pitfalls before they returned and Tori agreed to sign the paperwork. Jenkins then reached into this briefcase and withdrew a checkbook and wrote out a check, signing it with a flourish.

Tori took it from him, admiring all those zeros. "Thank you, Mr. Jenkins. I'm glad we could come to an agreement and save Bradley's reputation from harm."

That was a lie. If the guy would punch her, he was likely to punch other women—or worse—too. Or maybe—just maybe—if he was smarter than Tori gave him credit for—he might just learn his lesson.

Maybe.

Jenkins put the checkbook and pen away and stood.

"I'll show you to the door," Tori said.

As soon as the man was gone, Kathy let out a breath. "Well, that was a surprise."

Herb leaned back in his chair. "Well, not really," he said, sounding smug.

Tori took her chair again. "What did you do? And how did you get that video of Bradley attacking me."

"Let's just say I called in a few favors."

"From whom?" Kathy asked, also sitting down again.

"That's none of your business," Herb said. "But I figure that twenty-thousand dollar check means you won't have to substitute teach until boating season rolls around again."

"Did you think he'd go as high as twenty grand?" Tori asked skeptically.

"Let's just say I had an amount in mind, and you got maybe a little more than that."

Tori shook her head. "Thanks, Gramps."

"You're welcome. I know how hard you work—both of you gals—and I'll tell you what, if you find yourself short, you just ask me to help. Not for frivolous stuff." He looked them over. They were both dressed in what couldn't even be called workplace casual. They obviously didn't indulge in frivolous purchases. "Just if you need a little help."

"But Gramps, what will the rest of the family think? They're already convinced I bamboozled you into giving me the compound."

"They don't have to know."

Tori bit her lip. Irene was the world's biggest gossip. There were no secrets as far as she was concerned. And even though most of Tori's family lived far from Lotus Bay, they were bound to find out about Herb's generosity. Still, she crossed her fingers that they wouldn't. And anyway, with that twenty grand, Tori would do everything she could not to have to ask for a handout.

"It's just too bad that young man probably won't learn his lesson," Herb said, shaking his head.

"Well, that's where you're wrong, Mr. Cannon," Kathy said.

Herb looked from Kathy to Tori. "What have I missed."

"Well," Tori began. "What we didn't mention yesterday was that while Kath and I were at Tom's Grocery to buy the chicken, we saw Bradley stride through the store to the beer cooler."

Herb's lips began to curve into a smile. "Tell me more."

Kathy smirked. "Someone took out her phone and began recording the young man, who pulled a fake ID out of his wallet and paid for a twelve-pack."

"That was very smart of you, Kathy."

"Oh, it wasn't me," she said, and nodded in Tori's direction.

Tori shrugged. "And...it just so happens I sent Detective Osborn a copy of the video."

"Well, wasn't that handy," Herb said. His smile had graduated to a grin. "Just one thing," he said, sobering. "You hightail it to the bank and cash that check Jenkins gave you PDQ. You don't want them to put a stop on it and cheat you out of what you're owed."

"Yes, Gramps," Tori said dutifully.

Herb looked at the clock. "I've got just enough time to pick up Irene and get to the airport for check-in."

"Call me tonight and let me know you got in okay," Tori said.

"I will," Herb promised. He rose from his seat, gave both women a hug and kiss on the cheek, and headed out the door. Tori and Kathy followed. Waving as he pulled out of the lot.

Once the rental car disappeared, Kathy spoke. "You better go to the bank—and right now."

Tori saluted her roommate. "Yes, ma'am. Wanna come with me? I think we might hit Tom's Grocery and maybe buy a bag of shrimp and a couple of steaks."

"If nothing else, you can first put it against your cheek," Kathy advised. "For medicinal purposes, you understand."

"Oh, yes," Tori agreed.

"And shall we invite Anissa?"

"I don't see why not. She shares just about all our joys and sorrows."

Kathy grinned. "I'll make a wonderful salad, and we can have baked potatoes and—"

"Aren't you forgetting something?" Tori asked.

Kathy looked puzzled. "I don't think so."

"Technically, you still have a job at The Bay Bar."

"I just thought...."

"Neither Paul nor Noreen has told you not to show up this afternoon."

Kathy's expression darkened, and she let out a long, low breath. "Does this mean I have to call or go over there to find out?"

"At the least, you need to text one of them," Tori said,

knowing Kathy didn't have Paul's cell phone number. Either way, Noreen and Kathy were going to have to clear the air. After all, they were next-door neighbors. Things were bound to get even more awkward if they didn't address the events surrounding the bridal shower.

"What are you going to say to her?" Tori asked.

Kathy's eyes grew damp. "I don't know. I really don't know."

CHAPTER 19

Kathy accompanied Tori to the bank, where Tori deposited the twenty-thousand dollars, and took the tacked-on amount it had cost her to go to Urgent Care in cash. They bought the ingredients for a wonderful dinner but held off inviting Anissa until they knew if Kathy would be working that evening. Although if Kathy had her way, she'd be turning in her notice no matter what.

Still, it was just after two when Kathy screwed up her courage and walked across the road and entered The Bay Bar.

They usually stopped serving lunch by then, but there was no aroma of burgers and fries. A couple sat at one of the tables, but no one sat at the bar. A morose-looking Paul glanced up as Kathy entered the dining room.

"Hey," Kathy called.

"Hey," Paul answered without enthusiasm. "What's going on?"

"Well, I came in to see if I still have a job—and to pick up my paycheck," she added. If she was going to get screwed, she wasn't going to get screwed out of the money she'd earned working at the bar.

Paul reached below the bar and came up with a white, business-sized envelope. "Here's your check."

"And I take it it's my last."

Paul wouldn't meet her gaze. "Yeah."

Kathy accepted the envelope. "I think I deserve to know why?"

"Why I don't need you here?"

He'd said "I," not "we."

"Yeah."

"The kitchen's closed for a while."

Kathy blinked. "Oh?"

"Yeah. Noreen and I are taking a break."

"A break?" Kathy asked, a rush of guilt washing through her.

"Yeah. She packed a bag and left after the dinner service Saturday night. She said she had a lot to think about."

Boy, did she ever.

"I'm sorry, Paul. I didn't mean to cause you guys trouble."

"You didn't," he emphasized and then shook his head. "Noreen has always been jealous of my relationship with my sister. I don't understand it. But I'm grateful you gave Barb a happy day. God knows she deserved it. I figure I can hire someone to man the grill until or unless Noreen doesn't come back any time soon."

"Do you want her back?" Kathy asked.

"Right now, I can't stand the sight of her. I'm so friggin' angry. But I do love her. We might have to go to counseling to figure out if we'd still be good together. I'm willing to try, but man...she's gonna have to do some fancy talking to explain why she did what she did."

Kathy's gaze dipped to the oak bar. "Well, I'm sorry how things worked out."

Again, Paul shook his head. "No. This thing has been festering for a while. All I know is that in less than two weeks, my baby sister is getting married, and I'll be there to cheer her on. I won't be going with Noreen, no matter how things work out between us."

Kathy nodded, unwilling to increase the poor man's pain. She changed the subject. "Much as I love the bar as a customer, I don't feel like I'm a good fit as a server."

"That's too bad, you did really well. The customers like you, and you sure can upsell desserts."

Kathy almost blushed. "Thanks." She looked around the empty dining room. Without a line cook, the place wouldn't bring in the kind of cashflow it took to keep it a going concern. "Well, I'd better get going. If there's one silver lining to this situation, it's that two of Barb's friends have booked the weekend at Swans Nest."

"That's great," Paul said with a wan smile. "Maybe by then, I'll have someone in the kitchen who can feed them dinner."

"I'll cross my fingers for you."

Paul nodded, and Kathy left the bar, walking slowly back to the Cannon Compound.

Once inside the bungalow, she opened the envelope. Instead of one check, there were two, both signed by Paul: one for her work as a server, and one for the bridal shower. It pretty much covered all her costs.

Tori entered the kitchen. "Well, are you working?"

Kathy shook her head. "Noreen left Paul."

Tori's mouth dropped. "She what?"

Kathy nodded. "Packed a bag and left Saturday night. The kitchen's closed until he can find someone to man—or woman—the grill."

"Oh, man, that's terrible."

"Yeah."

"Does he blame you?"

"No. And," Kathy waved one of the checks in the air, "he paid me for the bridal shower."

"That man deserves a halo and wings."

"Yeah. So, why do I feel so crummy?"

"It's not your fault, Kath. Noreen decided to try to embarrass her sister-in-law in front of her friends and family. Instead, it blew up in her face. That's karma."

"I suppose."

"I guess we'll be heading back to the bank tomorrow."

"Yeah."

"In the meantime, I'll text Anissa and invite her for supper. It'll give me something to do while I wait for Detective Osborn."

"Why's he coming here? To talk about the video of Bradley buying beer?"

"That, and maybe something else."

"What?"

"Can't say—but I'll tell you all about it later."

Kathy scrutinized her friend's face. "What are you up to?"

Tori's eyes widened in feigned innocence. "Nothing...much. But I think I've put all the pieces together concerning Chuck Stanton's accident."

"And what are you going to do about it?"

"I'm not sure. But as soon as I figure it out, I'll let you know."

∽

HUDDLED IN HER JACKET, Tori strode to the top of her dock, her gaze taking in a c of Lotus Bay's western shore. She never tired of the sight.

She noted a solitary figure standing on the bridge, casting a line over the rails, fishing. With purpose, Tori circled her property and marched onto the bridge's wooden walkway, heading for its lone denizen.

"Hey, Eric. How's it going?"

Eric turned a sour look on her. "Like crap. I lost my job."

Tori stood next to him, settling her forearms on the wooden railing. A pair of swans slowly paddled toward the Cannon

Compound some ten yards off the bridge, looking serene. She often found the swans' placid visage made her feel calm, too, but she also knew that they could be fierce fighters if they or their cygnets felt threatened. "Yeah, Kathy lost her job at The Bay Bar, too. But I don't think it'll be long before they either hire a new cook or Noreen returns."

"Stupid woman," Eric muttered under his breath. "She obviously didn't think about the employees when she went off on vacation."

Was that how Paul was couching the situation or was he giving a different story to different people depending on how well he knew them? He'd certainly been honest with Kathy, and it wasn't Tori's place to give a different explanation.

"Yeah, and you were just getting started."

"Paul said he'd rehire me as soon as they got a new cook. I sure hope it's sooner rather than later."

Eric's line jerked, and he began reeling in his line.

"Casting for supper?" Tori asked.

"Yeah. I had big plans for the money I was going to earn at the bar—especially on weekends. Kathy said they did big business and that busboys got a percentage of the waitress's tips."

"Yeah, I know."

Eric shook his head as he wound in the last of his line. The perch attached to the hook wasn't worth keeping. "Damn," he swore, released the hook, and tossed the fish back into the water.

"Things have been tough for you these past couple of years," Tori said. It wasn't a question.

"I make out all right."

"Sounds like it, what with your fishing and the stuff you preserve from your garden."

"I've got twenty quarts of tomatoes, eight quarts of string beans, and all that summer squash in the freezer."

It sounded like a lot, but not if he expected to feed himself for the winter.

"Since you haven't had a job in a while, how do you keep up with all your bills?"

"I'm frugal," Eric said under his breath.

"I imagine you would be," Tori said, her gaze drifting over the water. It tended to calm down later in the day, even during the cooler months. But Mother Nature was fickle. The wind could pick up with little warning, turning the bay into a churning mass of white-capped waves.

"I noticed your wood pile was pretty low."

"Another week or two, and I could've bought a cord. It would be a stretch, but I could get through the winter on that."

It sounded like wishful thinking to Tori.

"Have you got an electric blanket for really cold nights?"

"Nah. I just boil up some water and fill my mom's old water bottle. You'd be surprised how warm you keep. I got me one of those sleeping bags that's good for down to zero degrees. I keep pretty warm."

Tori wondered how often that sleeping bag saw the inside of a washing machine.

Tori's gaze shifted to the Cannon Compound's parking lot. The lack of customers had kept it empty all day, but she had a feeling there'd soon be at least a couple more vehicles pull into the slots. Anissa, of course, and....

She thought about how to bring up a painful subject—and should it be her to do it?

She saw the battered pickup pull into her lot and made her decision to hurry things along.

"What happens when the power goes off at your place?"

Eric snorted an aborted laugh. "I toss more wood on the fire. Don't you?"

"I don't actually have a fireplace. I'm thinking about getting a generator."

"Too rich for my blood," Eric muttered.

"I took a walk yesterday along Resort Road—near my friend

Anissa's house. She told me about an abandoned orchard. She picks apples there and makes applesauce."

"Yeah. Behind the old Hanson place," Eric said. "I've picked up a bunch of the windfall apples before the deer can get to them. Nobody keeps it up. They'd just go to waste otherwise. Did you pick some, too?"

Tori shook her head. "I don't know how to can. I'd probably poison myself with botulism."

"Nah, canning is easy. You just have to make sure everything is sterilized."

Like his cruddy sleeping bag?

Tori nodded. "Friday night, me, my gramps, Kathy, and Anissa went to an auction in Warton."

"What's that got to do with apples?" Eric asked.

"While I was there, I spoke to the widow of the guy who was found in Anissa's boat last week."

Eric cast his line into the water, didn't wait for it to settle, and started reeling it back in.

"Yeah. It turns out he was quite the gambler. She was there selling off his fishing gear, hoping to pay off his gambling debts."

"Too bad for her," Eric said, whipped his pole over his shoulder, let loose the catch on the reel, and the line went flying northbound.

Anissa rounded the edge of the compound and stepped onto the bridge's walkway.

This was not what Tori had anticipated.

Go away, Tori mentally commanded, but Anissa didn't seem to pick up her psychic vibe and strode purposefully toward them.

"Hey, guys, what's up?" she called cheerfully.

"Not much," Tori said, her voice tight. She pulled out her phone and glanced at the time. It was dwindling. Maybe Anissa being there could be a good thing. Tori decided not to change her plans and plunged on.

"There's a rumor going around that Chuck Stanton was doing

illegal electrical hookups for people with no accounts with—or had been cut off by—the power company."

"Why would he do that?" Eric asked, checking his hook, finding it empty, and threaded a piece of earthworm through it. *He must be digging bait in his yard*, Tori mused. He sure wasn't buying it from her.

"That gambling debt hung over him like a huge weight," Tori said; she was once again spitballing all this.

"What's that got to do with me?" Eric asked.

"I didn't say it did," Tori said, "but now that you mention it...."

Eric's jaw tightened. He should have kept his mouth shut.

"I saw the wires behind the Hanson house were sagging with something that looked burned on them. I wonder if he fell from a ladder and instinctively reached for something—anything—to keep from falling some ten or fifteen feet to the ground."

"You'd have to ask the Hansons about that."

"Oh, I'm sure Detective Osborn will—if he hasn't already."

Eric's body tensed.

Anissa frowned. "Did he fall, or was he pushed?"

"Or did someone yank a ladder out from him?" Tori speculated.

Eric said nothing, casting once again.

"Even if that happened, someone would have to be awfully strong to haul a body from the top of Resort Road all the way to your dock," Anissa pointed out.

"Detective Osborn thought whoever did that would have to be mighty strong."

"That sounds logical," Anissa said.

"But really, all someone had to do was load the body into a vehicle of some kind and move it to my dock."

"That doesn't make sense," Anissa said, playing devil's advocate. "You couldn't get a car onto the far end of the dock. It's only four feet wide. Even a golf cart would be too big."

"How about a wheelbarrow?" Tori suggested.

Once again, Eric finished winding in his line, released the catch on his reel, flicked his wrist, and let out the line, without commenting.

"I still don't understand why someone picked *my* boat to dump the body," Anissa said, frowning.

"Well, I can," Tori said. She pointed toward her docks, where only a few scattered boats still graced the slips. Among them was Anissa's aluminum boat. "Yours is the furthest out. I only had two slips paid for the season in that area, and they were mothballed right after Labor Day. And the perfect vantage point for seeing that boat is right here on this bridge," Tori finished.

Silence greeted that statement.

Eric reeled in his line once more. "The fish just aren't biting today."

Out of the corner of her eye, Tori saw another vehicle pull into the compound's lot, parking next to Anissa's truck.

"So what do you know about Chuck Stanton's death?" Tori asked.

"I don't know a damn thing," Anissa muttered, and Tori turned to give her the evil eye.

"I don't know what you mean," Eric said.

"I think you do," Tori said. "There's an extra power line attached to the back of your house. It was spliced in from the big pole on the edge of Hanson's property. How much was Chuck Stanton charging you for that power cable?"

Eric reeled in his line. The piece of worm had fallen off the hook, which he attached to one of the line guides on his pole.

"I don't know what you mean," Eric said, picking up his empty bucket, and preparing to leave the bridge.

"Come on, Eric. Detective Osborn isn't a jerk. I'm sure he's already figured out the whole thing."

Eric's expression soured. "What was I supposed to do? I've got a whole freezer full of food that'll rot, and I'll starve over the winter if I don't have electricity!" he practically wailed. "A lot of the stuff I grew over the summer is in that freezer."

"Did you shake the guy off the ladder?" Anissa asked sternly.

"No! The asshole was screaming at me—telling me he'd turn me in for stealing power—he's the one who set the whole thing up! He kept asking for more. I didn't have the money, and he was gonna cut me off. And then his foot slipped on the ladder. I saw him fall, and heard him scream as he caught hold of the power line. What was I supposed to do? I mean, I did what I could. I shoved the ladder under him but it was too late. It was made of wood—non-conducting—and I kept pushing and pushing until the guy fell to the ground. He was dead. I got scared. I didn't know what to do, so I waited until it was dark and then ... then I figured I couldn't just leave him lying on the grass. He had a wedding ring. I figured he had somebody waiting for him. It was almost two in the morning before I loaded him into my wheelbarrow and took him down to your place. It took almost a whole day until you found him."

"After you dumped him in Anissa's boat, you drove his truck to Warton and left it in the municipal lot."

"Yeah," Eric muttered. "It was a long walk back home in the dark."

Yeah, it was a six-mile drive from Warton to the Cannon Compound.

"Why didn't you just call the police?" Tori pressed.

"And get in trouble?" he wailed.

"Oh, buddy, you're in loads more trouble than you would have been if you'd just called the cops right away," Anissa said.

"What do you mean?" Eric asked.

"You moved the body. Not only that, but you hid it. That's the concealment of a corpse," Tori said. "That alone can get you four years in prison."

Eric looked even more scared. "I did not kill that man."

"But you didn't report it, either," Tori accused. "And now you're going to jail."

Eric dropped the bucket and his fishing rod. "The hell I am," he yelled and took off, heading east across the bridge's walkway—and smacked right into Detective Osborn.

"Whoa!" the detective said, grabbing Eric by the shirt sleeve. "Where do you think you're going?"

Tori and Anissa sprinted to meet up with the two men.

"I take it you're Eric Mooney," Osborn said.

Eric said nothing, but Tori gave a nod.

Osborn spoke to Eric. "I'd like you to come down to headquarters for a little chat."

"I know my rights," Eric grunted.

Osborn raised an eyebrow. "And what rights do you think will be violated?" he asked evenly.

"I have a right to an attorney. And if I can't afford one, you have to provide one."

"Is that so?" Osborn said. "Well-versed in the law, are you?"

"I watch TV just like everybody else."

Yeah. If you watched crime TV shows, you were well versed in the Miranda rights phrasing.

"You got something to hide?" Osborn asked Eric.

Eric avoided the detective's gaze and said nothing.

"Why don't you sit in the back of my car for a bit while I talk to the ladies here."

Eric gave Tori a pleading look. While she felt sorry for him, she also knew what he'd done and the problems it had caused Anissa and Alice Stanton and tied up valuable time for the Ward County Sheriff's Department.

Eric didn't put up a struggle as Osborn led him to his unmarked police vehicle, putting him in the back seat without cuffing him.

Once the door closed shut, Osborn turned to the women.

"I'm assuming the guy spilled his guts to you ladies."

"Not exactly," Anissa said. She was always wary of law enforcement—and with good reason.

"I just deduced a few things, and Eric confirmed them," Tori explained.

"You wouldn't happen to want to tell me about it, would you?"

Tori glanced over Osborn's shoulder to see Eric glaring at her. She felt bad for the guy but she also felt bad for Alice Stanton, who'd loved her husband. That she'd had to accept his foibles after his death had probably taken the shine off that love, but still.

Anissa didn't look at Tori during her recitation of the facts. She might not have approved of her snitching to the cops, but doing so also cleared her name. Talk about a Catch 22.

"How much trouble is Eric in?" Tori asked at last.

"That's up to the county prosecutors. Maximum—maybe ten years in prison. Minimum—probation. It sure won't be up to me to figure that out."

"He's not a bad person," Tori said sincerely. "He's just broke. People do stupid things when they're caught between a rock and a hard place."

"You don't have to tell me that. I've been dealing with people in that situation my whole career," Osborn said with what Tori thought was sadness.

"Will you arrest him tonight?"

"Maybe. I've sent for a lab team and the power company to get samples from whatever is clinging to that power line."

"It's burned flesh," Anissa said flatly.

"Probably," Osborn agreed. He withdrew the keys to his SUV from his pocket. "I'll be wanting a statement from you ladies. Is sometime tomorrow all right?"

Tori glanced in her friend's direction. Anissa gave the barest of nods. "Yeah. Text or call me to know where and when."

"Will do," Osborn said. He climbed into his vehicle, but instead of heading back to his headquarters, he steered the SUV back up the Resort Road. No doubt he would wait for the lab team to arrive before taking Eric to be interrogated.

Anissa shook her head as they watched the SUV disappear. "We are now officially snitches," she muttered.

"What else can we do? And now you're in the clear," Tori reminded her.

"Yeah, but it doesn't feel good."

Tori sighed. "I know."

Tori turned and slowly walked back to where Eric had dropped his bucket and fishing rod. She'd take it back to his place the next morning and place it on his porch. And she wondered if he'd ever get to use them again.

CHAPTER 20

A dusting of snow sat on the boathouse deck's railing. A thin layer of ice stretched a few feet from the shore. Come January, it could be inches thick—enough to support the plethora of ice fishermen who flocked to the bay for the winter sport.

Tori surveyed the inside of her most recent renovation. Though the place wasn't yet heated, she'd been collecting furniture and the accouterments to outfit the place—with new and thrifted items. She'd buy the upholstered pieces closer to her grand opening in May—still six months away.

"It's looking pretty good," Kathy said from behind her.

Tori turned. "I didn't hear you come in."

"No, you were in La-La Land," Kathy said and laughed.

"Yeah." Tori smiled. "And isn't it pretty?"

"Show me everything," Kathy said. She'd been busy with guests at Swans Nest and was gearing up for another full house that weekend. Since the bridal shower two months before, Swans Nest had been booked solid on weekends, and Kathy had also had several weekday guests. She was back in the black and bursting with happiness. Since the settlement with Bradley Hughes's parents, Tori was feeling pretty perky herself.

Tori walked Kathy through the kitchen, where she'd stocked the cupboards with plates, glasses, bowls, and serving dishes—enough for six since that's what the boathouse could accommodate. New silverware graced a drawer, and a crock filled with cooking utensils sat on the counter, along with a microwave, coffee maker, toaster, and electric tea kettle. "All I need now are couches, some chairs, mattresses, and linens."

"That's fantastic," Kathy gushed.

"And now I get to do a lot of this all over again for the Lotus Lodge over the next few months."

"*You're* going to do it?" Kathy asked. "I thought your grandfather was taking care of all that."

"Yeah, he was. But I'd much rather do it myself because...."

Kathy frowned. "Because what?"

Tori sighed. "I kind of asked Gramps to take on another project instead."

"What? Do you want to buy more and bigger boats for your rental fleet?" Kathy asked.

Tori shook her head. "No, I asked Gramps to bail out Eric Mooney."

Kathy's expression darkened. "Why?"

"Because Gramps was friends with his folks. They were good customers for years. Eric might have made some really poor choices, but he's not a bad person. Just someone caught between a rock and a hard place."

"So what does that mean for Eric?"

"Gramps is paying Eric's bail so he can come home. He's also squaring everything with the electric company so that Eric will have power—at least through the winter. He's going to hire an attorney for Eric to hopefully get him probation instead of years in jail. If Eric is released, Gramps said he'll restock his freezer so he can get through the winter."

"That's very generous of Herb."

Tori sighed. "More like I pulled a guilt trip on him. Part of the deal is that Eric has to have a job and start to support himself. I talked to Paul, and he said he'd welcome Eric to come back to the bar to bus tables."

"That's hardly a lucrative position," Kathy remarked.

"No, but I had an idea...if you're willing to listen."

"Listen to what?" Kathy asked, an edge creeping into her voice.

"Eric is a wiz at growing veggies, and has a big backyard. What if he put up a little stand at the edge of your property and sold produce during the summer and fall? Maybe he could give you a deal on veggies to serve to your guests in lieu of payment. You know, the whole farm-to-table thing."

"I'm listening," Kathy said obliquely.

"I just think the guy was handed a crappy life, and if we can lift him up, what's the harm?"

Kathy seemed to think about what Tori had to say. "Yeah. I guess I could do that. I mean, there is room for cars to come and go at the bottom of my parking lot that shouldn't interfere with my visitors. And touting home-grown veggies would be a perk for my guests." She mulled it over for a bit more. "Okay. But Eric has to provide his own stand. That can't be up to me."

"I'm sure between Gramps and me, we can spare the lumber and have Anissa build a little covered stand."

"Okay, then, I guess I'm in."

Tori grinned. "Thanks."

"What about Mrs. Stanton?" Kathy asked. "How would she feel knowing Eric could get out of jail?"

Tori sobered. "I asked Detective Osborn about that."

"And?" Kathy inquired.

"She's nowhere to be found."

"What?"

"Their house has been sold, and she seems to have disappeared."

"To get away from the people her husband owed money to?" Kathy asked.

"Maybe."

"Well, one woman disappeared, and one has reappeared."

Tori frowned. "What do you mean?"

"Noreen's back."

Tori blinked. "You've spoken to her?"

Kathy shook her head. "But her car is back in The Bay Bar's parking lot."

"Maybe she came back to get some of her things," Tori posed.

"Paul and Noreen don't *live* at the bar," Kathy reminded her friend.

"Yeah. Sometimes I forget that. So, she's back behind the grill?" Tori asked.

Kathy shrugged. "Barb's wedding happened over a month ago. Paul said he wouldn't go with Noreen. Maybe they've patched things up now that that event has passed."

"Maybe," Tori remarked.

The boathouse's back door opened, and Anissa appeared. "There you guys are."

Tori laughed. "As you like to point out, we're not guys—we're women."

Anissa grinned. "That you are." She turned to Kathy. "Well, what do you think?"

"I think you *guys*," she emphasized the last word, "have done a fantastic job."

"Just wait until Tori finishes furnishing the Lotus Lodge."

"I'm going to have a lot of fun with that. Lots of kitschy decorations."

"Is that all you have left to do on the seven units?" Kathy asked.

"Well, the laundry room is next, but we're not getting into

that until the spring. It really only needs a facelift," Anissa explained.

"And new appliances—big boys that can handle all the linens," Tori said.

"I'm trying to talk Tori into buying a couple of vending machines, too," Anissa said. "Her gramps said back in the day they made out like bandits selling pop and candy."

"That was after my time spending summers here," Tori added. "After the little store around the corner closed."

"Just think, come May, we'll be starting a whole new season on Lotus Bay," Kathy said wistfully.

"It can't come soon enough," Tori muttered.

"I think we deserve to celebrate," Anissa said. "I brought some steaks, a few Russett potatoes, and bag of salad greens. They're already in the kitchen. What say we each take one of them and prepare us a feast?"

"Sounds good to me," Kathy said.

"And me," Tori echoed.

"Let's go," Anissa said, leading the way, but Tori paused for one last look at her favorite view: the sun setting over Lotus Bay.

KATHY'S RECIPES

Sun-Dried Tomato Muffins
Ingredients
½ cup all-purpose flour
¼ cup whole wheat flour
1 teaspoon baking powder
1 teaspoon granulated sugar
¼ teaspoon ground pepper
⅛ teaspoon salt
½ cup milk
2 tablespoons vegetable oil
2 to 3 tablespoons chopped pimiento-stuffed green olives
3 to 4 tablespoons chopped sun-dried tomatoes

Preheat the oven to 425ºF (220ºC, Gas Mark 7). Grease 12 (1 1/4-inch) mini muffin cups. Combine the flours, baking powder, sugar, pepper, and salt in a medium bowl. Whisk together the milk and oil in a small bowl; stir into the flour mixture until just moistened. Fold in the olives and tomatoes. Spoon equal amounts into the muffin cups. Bake for 15 minutes or until lightly browned. Serve warm

Yield: 12 mini muffins

Lemon Pound Cake

Ingredients
1 cup butter, softened
½ cup shortening
3 cups granulated sugar
5 large eggs
1 tablespoon grated lemon zest
1 tablespoon lemon extract
3 cups all-purpose flour
1 teaspoon salt
½ teaspoon baking powder
1 cup milk

Icing
¼ cup butter, softened
1¾ cups confectioners' sugar
2 tablespoons lemon juice
1 teaspoon grated lemon zest

Preheat the oven to 350ºF (180ºC, Gas Mark 4). In a large bowl, cream the butter, shortening, and sugar until light and fluffy, about 5 minutes. Add the eggs, one at a time, beating well after each addition. Stir in the lemon zest and extract. Combine the flour, salt, and baking powder; gradually add to the creamed mixture alternately with the milk. Beat just until combined. Pour into a greased 10-in. bundt pan. Bake for 70 minutes or until a toothpick inserted in the center comes out clean. Cool for 10 minutes before removing it from the pan to a wire rack to cool completely. In a small bowl, combine the icing ingredients; beat until smooth. Spread over the top of the cake.

Yield: 12-16 servings

Poppy Seed Lemon Scones

Ingredients

2 cups all-purpose flour
5 tablespoons granulated sugar, plus 1 teaspoon
1 tablespoon baking powder
1 teaspoon salt
1 teaspoon vanilla extract
¼ teaspoon lemon extract
¼ teaspoon almond extract
⅔ cup half-and-half, plus 1 tablespoon (divided)
Zest of one lemon (approximately 1 tablespoon)
1 tablespoon lemon juice
1½ tablespoons poppy seeds
6 tablespoons chilled butter, cut into small pieces
Lemon icing (optional—see below)

Preheat the oven to 425°F (220°C, Gas Mark 7). In a bowl, whisk together the flour, baking powder, sugar, poppy seeds, lemon zest, and salt. Cut in the butter with a pastry blender or two knives until the mixture resembles coarse crumbs. Stir in the half-and-half, extracts, and lemon juice until just moistened. On a lightly floured surface, knead dough gently 5 to 10 times. Pat into a 1-inch-thick round. Cut into 8 wedges; place on a parchment-lined baking sheet, 2" apart. Brush the tops with 1 tablespoon half-and-half, then sprinkle each scone top with sugar. Bake until golden brown, 12 to 15 minutes. Cool on a wire rack.

Yield: 8 scones

Optional Lemon Icing

Ingredients

1 cup of confectioners' sugar
1 tablespoon fresh lemon juice
¼ teaspoon lemon extract

KATHY'S RECIPES

½ teaspoon vanilla extract
1 tablespoon half-and-half or heavy cream

In a small bowl, combine all the ingredients to form a lemon glaze to drizzle over the tops of the scones, or to dip the scones in the icing. Let sit on a wire rack to set.

Yield: 8 scones

ABOUT THE AUTHOR

The immensely popular Booktown Mystery series is what put Lorraine Bartlett's pen name Lorna Barrett on the New York Times Bestseller list, but it's her talent—whether writing as Lorna, or L.L. Bartlett, or Lorraine Bartlett—that keeps her in the hearts of her readers. This multi-published, Agatha-nominated author pens the exciting Jeff Resnick Mysteries as well as the acclaimed Victoria Square Mystery series, the Tales of Telenia adventure-fantasy saga, and now the Lotus Bay Mysteries, and has many short stories and novellas to her name(s). Check out the descriptions and links to all her works, and sign up for her emailed newsletter here: https://www.lorrainebartlett.com

If you enjoyed *After the Tempest*, please help spread the word by reviewing it on your favorite online review site. Thank you!

Connect with Lorraine Bartlett on Social Media

ALSO BY LORRAINE BARTLETT

Writing as Lorraine Bartlett

THE LOTUS BAY MYSTERIES

Panty Raid (A Tori Cannon-Kathy Grant mini mystery)

With Baited Breath

Christmas At Swans Nest

A Reel Catch

After The Tempest

The Best From Swans Nest (A Lotus Bay Cookbook)

Life On Lotus Bay (Box set)

THE VICTORIA SQUARE MYSTERIES

A Crafty Killing

The Walled Flower

One Hot Murder

Dead, Bath and Beyond (with Laurie Cass)

Yule Be Dead (with Gayle Leeson)

Murder Ink (with Gayle Leeson)

A Murderous Misconception (with Gayle Leeson)

Dead Man's Hand (with Gayle Leeson)

A Lethal Lake Effect

LIFE ON VICTORIA SQUARE

Carving Out A Path

A Basket Full of Bargains

The Broken Teacup

It's Tutu Much

The Reluctant Bride

Tea'd Off

Life On Victoria Square Vol. 1

A Look Back

Tea For You (free download in most countries)

Davenport Designs

A Ruff Week

Recipes To Die For: A Victoria Square Cookbook

Tales From Blythe Cove Manor

A Dream Weekend

A Final Gift

An Unexpected Visitor

Grape Expectations

Foul Weather Friends

Mystical Blythe Cove Manor

Blythe Cove Seasons (free download in most countries)

Tales of Telenia

(adventure-fantasy)

STRANDED

JOURNEY

TREACHERY

Short Women's Fiction

Love & Murder: A Bargain-Priced Collection of Short Stories

Happy Holidays? (A Collection of Christmas Stories)

An Unconditional Love

Love Heals

Blue Christmas

Prisoner of Love

We're So Sorry, Uncle Albert

Sabina Reigns (a novel)

WRITING AS L.L. BARTLETT
THE JEFF RESNICK MYSTERIES

Murder On The Mind

Dead In Red

Room At The Inn

Cheated By Death

Bound By Suggestion

Dark Waters

Shattered Spirits

Shadow Man

JEFF RESNICK'S PERSONAL FILES

Evolution: Jeff Resnick's Backstory

A Jeff Resnick Six Pack

When The Spirit Moves You

Bah! Humbug

Cold Case

Spooked!

Crybaby

Eyewitness

A Part of the Pattern

Abused: A Daughter's Story

Off Script

Writing as Lorna Barrett

The Booktown Mysteries

Murder Is Binding
Bookmarked For Death
Bookplate Special
Chapter & Hearse
Sentenced To Death
Murder On The Half Shelf
Not The Killing Type
Book Clubbed
A Fatal Chapter
Title Wave
A Just Clause
Poisoned Pages
A Killer Edition
Handbook For Homicide
A Deadly Deletion
Clause of Death
A Questionable Character
A Controversial Cover
A Perilous Plot

With The Cozy Chicks

The Cozy Chicks Kitchen
Tea Time With The Cozy Chicks
The Cozy Chicks Picnic (free download)